Tria and the Great Star Rescue

TRiA and the GReat StAr Rescue

REBECCA KRAFT RECTOR

Delacorte Press

Published by
Delacorte Press
an imprint of
Random House Children's Books
a division of Random House, Inc.
1540 Broadway
New York, New York 10036

Visit us on the Web! www.randomhouse.com/kids
Educators and librarians, for a variety of teaching tools, visit us at
www.randomhouse.com/teachers

Library of Congress Cataloging-in-Publication Data
Rector, Rebecca Kraft.
Tria and the great Star rescue / Rebecca Kraft Rector.
    p.   cm.
Summary: On the planet Chiron, a girl who has been afraid to venture
Outside must face germs and other frights when her mother and her
holographic best friend, Star, are kidnapped.
ISBN 0-385-72941-3
[1. Holography—Fiction. 2. Kidnapping—Fiction. 3. Fear—Fiction.
4. Friendship—Fiction. 5. Science fiction.] I. Title.
PZ7.R24453 Tr 2002
[Fic]—dc21

                                                          2001041749

The text of this book is set in 12.5-point Garamond.

Book design by Patrice Sheridan

Manufactured in the United States of America

February 2002

10 9 8 7 6 5 4 3 2 1

BVG

For my family,
who believed in me

chapter one

My fingers shook as I reached for a new handhold in the slippery rock. Below me, the cliffs plunged into the sea. Crashing breakers churned up a white froth of foam.

"You can do it, Tria!" Star called.

But I couldn't. My hand lost its grip, my feet slipped, and I plummeted down, arms windmilling.

With a thud I landed on the sofa.

Oof! I rolled over and pulled off the AlmostReality headband. Star knelt beside me on the sofa, looking worried. My best friend wasn't a climber. She preferred to sink herself into her studies.

"Are you okay?" she asked. She was wearing Borgarian gauzy purple pants and an embroidered sleeveless jacket. Our tutor, Mr. Willoughby, had been teaching us about the planet Borgar, which is best known for its outlandish clothing. "You were really high on the wall."

I glanced at the gel strip that covered the back wall of our pod, and tried to estimate where I'd been. "I did get a lot higher this time, didn't I?" I loved these virtual adventures. Once I'd even climbed the famous Supoorian banyan tree. "I hope Mom brings another AR game back from her travels."

Star stared into my eyes like a doctor. "You're looking a little disoriented. We'd better do something quiet for a while."

"Okay." I took off the rest of my AR gear and settled on the living room floor. My heart was still racing and my hands were sweaty. AlmostReality games were so good I felt like I'd just fallen off the real Cliffs of Redvor. I wiggled my bare toes in the tufted carpet. My tense muscles relaxed.

"Cards, please. Go Fish," Star said, dropping down beside me.

"Not that game!" I protested as the holo cards appeared and dealt themselves out. There was a glitch in our copy. "At least take the queens out."

Star grinned. "They're the best part."

"You just like to remind me of my mistakes," I said grumpily.

We fished back and forth, and it wasn't long before Star announced, "I only have one card left, Tria. Once I match it with the other three, I win!" She swung one slippered foot in time to the bells and cymbals of the Borgarian music she'd put on.

I took a guess. "Got any fives?"

Star twirled a finger through her violet hair and smiled. "Go fish."

Rats. "Fish," I said, and a card winked into existence in front of me. A nine. I didn't need any nines.

Star sat up and her card moved with her. Her eyes were dancing. "Got any queens?"

I groaned. "Ye-es," I said, dragging the word out reluctantly. Two of my three queens jumped out of line and spun smartly over to Star.

"Go on," I said to the third queen. "Get over there." It didn't move, and Star giggled. "Go!" I poked it, but my finger went right through the holo card. The queen still didn't move.

Star collapsed on the floor, holding her stomach and laughing madly.

I pretended to be angry. "You're never going to let me live this down, are you?"

When we were seven I had decided to reprogram the Go Fish playing cards. I've always liked to tinker with things and figure out how they work, especially holograms. Back then I thought it was a great idea to make the cards move only when you said, "Pretty please with sugar on top." Star figured out my trick right away. When Mom returned from off-planet, she made me put the cards back the way they'd been.

"Reprogramming so you'll win is called cheating," Mom had said.

"I wasn't cheating!" I had mumbled. "I just thought it would be fun to trick Star."

"Fix it."

I did my best. But putting things back the way they were was so boring. And things never seemed to work the same again. Like the queen of hearts.

"Pretty please with sugar on top," I muttered. The queen of hearts did a back flip and zipped over to join the others. I watched in disgust as the four queens spun in a happy circle before settling on the floor in a neat spread.

"I win!" Star said through her giggles. "I just love that queen of hearts."

"You win," I agreed. "Cards off." I watched with satisfaction as the queens and the rest of the cards disappeared. I loved seeing my mistakes vanish.

"One day," I said, "I'm going to be a great inventor and never make mistakes."

"And someday I'll be a famous ornithologist," said Star.

Star loved birds, all birds, any birds. Mom was going to help me buy a parrot hologram for Star's birthday. No one knew when Star's real birthday was, so we celebrated on the anniversary of the day she came to live with us.

"I'll have to do field research," Star said, rolling over and propping her head on one elbow. "Go Outside, visit lots of planets . . . study the bird populations of the galaxy."

I shuddered. "You don't want to go Outside. You can learn from holo vids."

Star frowned. "Lots of people live Outside, Tria. Don't you ever long to feel the wind in your hair? The warm sun on your face?" She tossed back her hair and lifted her heart-shaped face to an imaginary sun.

"No," I said firmly, squashing a sudden memory of playing on a sunny beach with Mom and Dad. "Lots of people live safely in their pods, just like us."

I looked around our living room, drawing comfort from the familiar surroundings. The walls curved softly around us, but we had built in features that added corners and odd angles. A shiny fractal trellis led to the overhead loft where I kept my experiments, and Mom's smaller artifacts nestled on the shelving underneath. Across the dull red tiles at the other end of the pod were the set of puff chairs and the large Olympian vase Mom had brought back from her last dig. And, of course, the sofa, with its cheerful turquoise and yellow colors, stood near the gel wall, perfectly positioned for me to fall onto its plump cushions. It was all just as it should be, safe and familiar.

Star moved close to me. "Just because your dad died Outside doesn't mean—"

I clapped my hands over my ears. "I don't want to talk about it."

My parents were archaeologists, and I had always gone on their digs when I was younger. So I was there when Dad caught a germ and got sick. "Just a flu," Mom had said lightly. "That's what we get for working around real people." Dad got better fast. But he was still weak when he went back Outside, and an Omegan slither spud bit him. And he died. Just like that.

I'd never gone Outside again. Dad wouldn't have died if we'd stayed inside. I hated that Mom was still an archaeologist. She kept telling me she was safe, that there were biopreventives for almost everything.

Besides, she reminded me, she had to make money for us to live on. So she went and I stayed in our pod here on Chiron.

"You can go Outside on Chiron, Tria," my mother had urged. "All the flora and fauna are well known and cataloged. It's perfectly safe."

But I didn't budge. Star came to live with me and be my best friend, and Mr. Willoughby became my Home Tutor.

Mr. Willoughby. Hmmm.

Star never went Outside because *I* never went Outside. She'd never be a famous ornithologist at this rate.

I uncovered my ears. "Star, why don't you go watch your bird holo vids? I have some work to do with Mr. Willoughby."

Star eyed me suspiciously. "You never want to do lessons."

I raised my eyebrows. "I like to learn new things."

"Right." Star didn't seem convinced, but she got up anyway. "I'll watch the vid in the bedroom then, and you can work out here."

"Thanks." I watched Star walking into the bedroom, her long violet hair cascading down her back. As she turned the corner, her elbow slid right through the doorway. "Clumsy," I heard her mutter.

I had a mission. I was never going Outside, but I didn't want to hold Star back. She should be able to feel the wind in her hair and the sun on her face and watch real birds in a real sky. She should be able to go wherever she wanted even when I wasn't there with my holo projector.

My mission? To make my best friend—my hologram friend—solid.

chapter two

"Now, if I remove this cell flat . . ."

I sat on the carpet surrounded by pieces of Mr. Willoughby. I scooped up some of the smaller bits and stuffed them into Mom's huge Olympian vase. It was a good thing Mom was off-planet again. She would not like what I'd done.

I powered up my WonderTool and inspected a chunk. Just then Star walked in and shrieked. "No, Tria! Not Mr. Willoughby!"

My hand jerked and I zapped a red wire. "Ow!" I popped my burned finger into my mouth and gave Star a reproachful look. "You don't have to scream."

It had been a good one—really loud and screechy. Star's programming allowed her to grow and change just like a real girl. This scream had sounded even better than some of her earlier ones.

"No need to fuss," I said, shaking my burned finger at her. "I'll put Mr. Willoughby back together."

Star clutched her hair. "Think, Tria! If you don't have Mr. Willoughby for your Home Tutor, you might have to go to an Outside school."

"Don't say that!" I shivered. Those Back to Basics schools were horrible. Some unlucky kids on Chiron actually left their pods and sat in rooms surrounded by other human beings. I could hardly stand to think about it.

"Besides, I'm doing this for you, Star! Once I figure out how things work, I'm going to make you real." Not alive, of course. Live people died. Or went away and left you alone. Or were mean, like that kid Mom invited over when she was still trying to get me to play with real people.

"I *am* real." Star sat down beside me. Her legs slid right through a sturdy circuit cube.

"Nobody can tell you're not human," I agreed, shifting the cube. "But I want to make you solid. Then you won't need a projector." I glanced up at her and then away. "And you could go Outside to see real birds and feel the wind in your hair and the sun on your face."

Star shook her head. "Tria, that's what I want for *you*. It's impossible to make a hologram solid. Be-

10

sides"—she fluffed her violet hair—"I'm perfect just the way I am. I can still study birds. And if I were solid, I'd have to take time to eat and use the residence cleaner—well, I would if you hadn't taken it apart—and I'd probably have to pick up these pieces, too." She scrambled to her feet. "You'd better put Mr. Willoughby back together right now, before your mother finds out."

I eased apart a series of Mr. Willoughby's chip strips. "I have two weeks before Mom gets home. And you know she never calls when she's off-planet. It's too expensive."

"Incoming call. Incoming call."

I jumped, and the strips flew out of my hand. Star and I gaped at each other. It had to be Mom. We didn't know any other people.

"You answer it while I hide Mr. Willoughby."

Star rolled her eyes. "I don't think you can."

Star was right. Mr. Willoughby was everywhere.

"Incoming call. Incoming call."

I covered my face. Mom was going to kill me. Oh well, better get it over with. I sighed and dropped my hands. "Answer holo phone."

Mom appeared in the middle of the room. She was biting a fingernail and looking over her shoulder. She turned to face us, and I was pleased to see the gold filigree earrings I'd given her swinging against her pale cheeks. The earrings had little hand-made glass balls on them—handmade, can you imagine?—and Mom really loved them. But then I noticed how exhausted she looked. There were dark shadows under her eyes and a livid red scratch across her chin. Mom was often dirty and messy, but she'd never looked like this before.

"Tria! Star! Thank goodness! I was afraid I was too late! Listen carefully—"

She broke off, and I knew she'd seen Mr. Willoughby.

I leaped to my feet and tried to stand in front of the worst of the mess. *Crunch.*

Oops! I stepped back hastily. *Crunch.*

I decided not to move.

"I *am* too late!" Mom pushed her tangled hair out of her face and peered at me. "Are you all right? They didn't hurt you, did they?"

She wasn't making sense. I often wished Mom were a hologram so I could examine her programming. Maybe then I'd understand her better.

"We're fine, Mom." I shifted uneasily from one foot to the other. "I'll fix Mr. Willoughby. He'll be as good as new."

Mom shook her head. "At least you and Star are

all right. You have to get out of there. As soon as I disconnect, get Star's disk and take the first scooter to South Back to Basics School. They're expecting you and you'll be safe there. The movers will pack up everything and send it after you."

What? "No, Mom, not an Outside school!" I took an unthinking step forward. *Crunch.* "I'll fix Mr. Willoughby, I promise."

Mom shook her head impatiently. "I'm sending Star vital information." Mom glanced over her shoulder again. "I need your help. When—"

My mother disappeared.

"Mom! Call reconnect! Reconnect!" Nothing happened.

"She's been cut off!" Star's violet eyes were wide. "But I received the message. We're in big trouble. No time to explain. Turn me off and keep me safe until we're at that school. Then find a holo projector as fast as you can."

"But Star, I'm not going Outside to a school with real people." Then it hit me. "Turn you off?"

I had never turned Star off. Never. I knew she was just a projection of light. It wouldn't hurt her. But with Mom gone so much, Star was all I had. Except for Mr. Willoughby, and he didn't count since he was my tutor.

"Hurry, Tria!"

"You're talking crazy! So is Mom! I'm not turning you off and I'm not going to that school." I folded my arms and stuck my chin in the air.

"Tria, it's a matter of life or death."

A sick feeling started in my stomach, and my legs turned all rubbery. Star was programmed to be practical. If she said "life or death," she meant *life or death.*

"Mom's in danger?" I whispered. That would be worse than being sent to school, even worse than turning Star off.

The pod entry chimed and I whirled to stare at it, my heart beating fast.

"Your mom's in danger and so are we," Star said. "Quick, turn me off and get us on the next scooter."

I went to the projection cabinet and slowly reached in. I knew exactly which switch controlled Star's disk, though I'd never touched it before.

Star and I looked into each other's eyes. I could tell she was scared, too. I swallowed hard. "I can't."

"You can. You must."

Closing my eyes, I reached for the switch. No. That was cowardly. I had to help Star through this. I opened my eyes.

Star smiled at me, her mouth crinkling at the corners. She lifted her hand and poked a finger at me. "Go. Pretty please with sugar on top."

I choked. Somewhere between laughter and tears, I nodded and flipped the switch.

And Star winked out.

chapter three

Ringggg! The pod entry chimed again.

I snatched Star's silver disk out of the projector and ducked into the bedroom. I flattened myself against the wall, trying to make myself as small as possible. Who was out there? Mom had mentioned movers. But maybe it was someone else. Someone Mom hadn't had a chance to tell us about.

"What am I supposed to do now?" I whispered to Star's disk. It lay small and silent in my palm. How was I going to do anything without Star?

Then I remembered her words: "We're in danger and so is your mom." I wasn't helping Mom by hiding in here. I grabbed a pair of shoes and put one on. Then I dropped Star's disk into the other shoe and shoved my foot in on top of it. Star should be safe there. My hands started shaking, and I fought back tears. Mom's danger didn't seem quite real, but Star's did. I could easily lose her Outside. I wished I could make a zillion copies of the disk, but that would be like trying to copy a human being. You could never capture all that evolving intelligence in the same form again.

But I wasn't going to lose her. I rubbed my eyes fiercely. "Don't worry, Star. You'll be safe."

I marched over to the entry and ran my tongue over dry lips. "Door open."

A woman wearing a green jumpsuit and sturdy work boots grinned at me. "Express Movers. Pod packup is our profession." She pushed her orange EM cap back on her head. "Have to say that. It's our slogan. Call me Em."

I let my breath out in a whoosh.

"You Tria?" She eyed me curiously. "Here's your commuter scooter ticket. Better hurry. It's due any minute."

"Th-thanks," I stammered. I took the ticket and edged around her to the open door. "Um, where do I go?"

She winked at me. "First trip? No need to be nervous. Just stand in front of the building. The scooter will stop when it detects your ticket."

I thanked her again and saw her do a double take

when she saw the pieces of Mr. Willoughby. I felt a little pang of guilt. No time to put him back together now. I had to leave.

I clenched my fists and stepped through the doorway. *This isn't so bad,* I told myself. But I wasn't Outside yet. A narrow corridor stretched in front of me and I tiptoed down it, past door after door. It gave me the shudders to think I lived near so many real people. At the descender I said, "Street level," just the way they did on the vids.

When the doors opened again, I stood there, heart thumping, mouth dry. My stomach churned. I couldn't go Outside with real people and germs and bugs and dangerous weather.

Outside . . . where people died.

Cool air blew in, bringing with it strange smells and sounds. I didn't know whether to cover my nose against the rank odors or put my hands over my ears to protect them against the whistles and clanks, the thumping feet and roaring voices. . . .

There were people everywhere! Big, small, fat, thin, hurrying, strolling, standing. Too many for me to count. Too many for me to believe! They couldn't all be real, could they?

And then one *touched* me. I squeaked in alarm.

"Sorry. Did I startle you?" The woman frowned as I cringed. "Are you Tria? I'm Zell, and this is Chip." The man behind her pushed a lock of black hair out of his eyes and nodded.

"We're Mammoth Movers. We're here to pack up your holographic equipment. Do you have any disks or projectors on you? It's not safe to take them on scooters, you know."

I shook my head. I was still trying to get used to being Outside, and my brain didn't seem to be working right. Something was wrong.

"Express Movers!" I said. "You should be from Express Movers." I looked down at Zell's old-fashioned green lace-up shoes. "You're dressed just like Em except for those shoes."

Chip loomed over me. "Do you have any disks or projectors?"

With a low purr, a sleek silver transport glided to a stop in front of my building. It was bigger than my whole pod. The scooter! Its air cushions pulsed gently against the ground. *Just like in the vids,* I thought, hypnotized by the realness of it, the size of it, the barely visible dimpling on the surfaces where the solar cells lay. . . .

"Well?" Zell's fingers closed around my arm.

"Get your germy fingers off me!" I screamed, shocked out of my fascination with the scooter. I tried to pull away, but she hung on.

"*Passengers enter here,*" an automated voice said.

Her fingers pressed in, hurting me. "Do you have any disks?" She shook my arm again and bent close.

Her breath was in my face. Moist and warm with zillions of germs. And it smelled! *Star, what should I do?* I thought frantically.

Suddenly I remembered something I'd seen on a holo vid. I stopped trying to pull away and stepped closer. Then I lifted my foot and brought it down hard on her green lace-ups.

"Ow!" She let go of me and bent over to clutch her toes.

"*Passengers enter here.*"

The man hovered close to her shoulder. "Are you hurt? Zell, are you hurt?"

Now was my chance to get back to the safety of my pod. But Mom needed me. I took a deep breath, put my head down, and dashed through the opened doors of the commuter scooter. "It's just like a moving pod," I kept repeating as the doors closed behind me. "Nice and safe."

An official-looking man took my ticket and fed it into a slot. "Sit anywhere," he said.

I swallowed hard. "Can being on a scooter hurt a holographic disk?"

He laughed. "Nothing hurts a disk."

I sighed in relief. That's what I'd thought, but I'd never been on a scooter before. Who knew what was okay and what wasn't?

I collapsed into an empty seat and shut my eyes tight. Zell and Chip weren't real movers. They must have been after Star, and Mom's "vital information."

I slowly opened my eyes. I didn't like this scooter. Everyone was jammed together, with walls curving in so close you could touch the ceiling if you stretched on tiptoe. Voices murmured, engines pulsed, and air hit my nose with a chemical tang. My breath came short and fast. There wasn't enough air in here. Too many people were breathing.

Calm down, I ordered myself. *You've had all the bio-preventives for Chiron. You're perfectly safe.* I wiggled my toes on Star's disk for courage. It wasn't so bad if I pretended the people were holograms.

The scooter stopped and started. People came and went. I actually dozed off and was jerked awake by the automated voice announcing, *"South Back to Basics School."*

Jumping to my feet, I hurried out the door, glancing over my shoulder to make sure no one was following me. When I faced forward again, the sun flashed in my eyes. I squinted and looked around. No busy streets or crowded pod buildings. Just a dusty red sand clearing, thorny bushes, and scrubby trees. And an endless brown wall.

The scooter lifted, whirling the sand up around me. Granules flew into my face and I coughed, trying to spit the grit from my mouth. But my mouth was as juiceless as a squeezed-out redfruit. Sand stuck to my damp face. I hadn't been this hot since I'd taken apart the atmosphere controller.

"Door open," I croaked at the wall. "Open." Nothing happened. How did people get in?

The wall seemed to stretch from horizon to horizon. Back to Basics School must be enormous, I decided as I trudged along, shielding my eyes from the sun and looking up to the jagged top of the barrier. And then, higher still, I saw something soaring on a breeze. A bird! A real bird in a real sky!

For a moment my fears disappeared. White

clouds stood out crisply against a vast dome of intense blue. I'd forgotten how beautiful Outside could be. The bird soared and swooped, and I was caught up in its joy, in its freedom, imagining the wind on its wings, the sun on its face. "Look, Star," I whispered.

I watched, hoping it would come lower so I could see the details of its feathers, claws, and beak, just like Mr. Willoughby had taught us. I wanted to be able to tell Star everything.

Then the bird glided away and I sighed. Suddenly I remembered where I was. "You're lucky that bird didn't attack you," I muttered. There was no telling what real creatures might do. Quickly I looked up into the sky again. It was empty, but I had to get out of here. My pulse pounded, sweat poured down my face, and I clenched and unclenched my fingers, looking again for an opening in the wall.

A movement in the corner of my eye caught my attention. A big black air taxi floated down, landing beside the trees—at least I assumed it was one of those taxis I'd read about. I didn't keep up with all the types of transport vehicles. All I cared about now was getting into this one.

I started toward the taxi, stumbling on the uneven sand.

The taxi door popped open, and two people climbed out. One was wearing green shoes. And pointing a stunner at me.

I spun around and lurched away across the sand. "Door open!" I yelled at the wall. "Open! Open!"

chapter four

The wall opened up. It was a miracle. I dashed through, and it closed solidly behind me. No laser beams blasted, no shouts pursued me.

I was safe. But I was still Outside.

Gasping, I bent over. Each breath scorched through my lungs like a flicker of flame. Trickles of wetness ran down my face. I couldn't move another inch. I'd been right all along. Outside was horrible! And I hadn't even known about the crooks chasing you, sand sticking to you, the sun blazing down on you. "I want to go home!" I cried out.

"What's wrong with you? We're only a minute late meeting the scooter."

A yellow-haired girl was looking down her freckled nose at me. Her hair shone with the shiny brightness of a krylar ball I'd once had, and I wondered dizzily whether she'd bounce if she fell on her head. A moon-faced boy in a floppy white hat stood at her shoulder. He wore a pale green T-shirt identical to the girl's. Behind them huge red mounds rose out of the sand, and after I blinked away the haziness, I realized they were school buildings.

"It is the sunstroke, Dayla!" The boy reached to his waist, where he had some kind of utility belt. A pouch, a perforated box, and a variety of tools hung from it. He stretched out his hand to me, and the belt clinked as he moved.

I flinched. These two looked like holograms, but they were probably real. Was this one going to grab me?

"She's afraid of you, Brash," the girl jeered. "Usually it's the other way around."

The boy stopped abruptly. Under the hat his round face turned red and his hand fell to his side.

"Is this your first time Outside, too?" I asked him, relaxing a little. "Isn't it awful? Let's go in."

"He grew up Outside," the girl scoffed with a toss of her hair. "On one of those dots of a farm in the

26

middle of nowhere. No people, no technology, just herds and herds of furbeasts."

I stared at him. "No technology? No holos, no atmosphere controllers, no Home Tutor . . . ?"

Brash shook his head and kicked at the sandy dirt.

"Listen up, New Girl." Dayla put her face right up to mine. Her nose was so close I could count its freckles. "My father sent me away so the Cruxor ambassador wouldn't be so angry. But as soon as I do something he can be proud of, I know my father will let me come home."

A rush of sympathy filled me. "I want to be at home, too."

"Then go home!" Dayla snarled.

I jerked back in surprise. Trying to talk to real people was like touching a green wire and having it change in your hand into a hot, sparking red one.

"I have to win ArborQuest," Dayla barked. "It's my chance to make my father proud. You'll just hold me back. Go home, you hear me?"

I stiffened. I didn't know what ArborQuest was and I didn't care. I'd had enough. I was Outside, hot, thirsty, and sweaty. Bad guys were chasing me, Mom was in danger, and my best friend was a disk in my shoe.

"Of course I hear you!" I exploded. "Your mouth is so big a planet could fit in there. Now move so I can get inside."

Dayla's jaw dropped and she backed up a step. Brash laughed softly. Dayla snapped her mouth shut.

"Shut up, Brash!" she yelled. "I'm going to have enough trouble winning with you on my team. I'm not having this fluff-brain loser, too."

Brash hunched his shoulders and stopped laughing. The life went out of him like a popped soap bubble. I lifted my chin. You had to stand up to bullies. My first "Bert the Bully" holo taught me that.

"Brash and I don't want *you* on *our* team!" I announced, hoping it was true. It felt good to yell at Dayla. In fact, it was the most fun I'd had since I took apart Mr. Willoughby. I was ready to blast her again when a voice commanded, "Brash! Dayla! Bring in the new student immediately."

"Remote announcer," Brash mumbled without meeting my eyes. "The Administrator."

Dayla scowled. "I'm not finished with you." She turned and marched off toward the mound-shaped buildings.

Brash's eyes flicked up at me and down again. He held out his hand. "It is water."

Water? The inside of my mouth was as gritty and hot as the sand around us. I ran a dry tongue over my parched lips and studied Brash. He was real, so he was crawling with germs. But I was about to collapse. I needed water if I wanted to get into that building. Slowly I reached for his hand.

Brash dropped a little bubble into my palm. "Roll it in your mouth."

I did as he said, and the bubble burst on my tongue. Cool water trickled down my throat. "Thank you!"

Brash smiled. "Come."

Panting, I plodded across the sand after Brash and into the biggest building. Dayla was tapping her foot. "You two are slowpoke losers."

I took a long, deep breath. All my muscles relaxed. The white walls of the corridor weren't at all like my pod, but at least I wasn't Outside. This inside air was as cool as Brash's water bubble. I loved atmosphere controllers! I'd never take another one apart. Or if I did, this time I'd put it back together.

Dayla led us down the hall and into a room on

the left. A slim man with freckled skin and close-cropped red hair leaned back in his execuchair and looked us over. A Back to Basics emblem—an intertwined B2B—was on the front of his navy blue jumpsuit. He raised his bushy eyebrows and shot a piercing glance at Dayla.

"Quarreling again, Dayla? And where is your hat? You're going to get sunstroke." He sighed and shook his head. "And Brash. You know I've asked you not to wear that survival belt. Yes, I've certified it technology free," he said as Brash placed a protective hand on his belt. "But you don't need it here."

Brash stared at the floor but his voice came loud and clear. "It is needed. Even here." He lifted his eyes for a moment and looked at me.

I thought of the water bubble and nodded at him. He smiled slightly and returned to studying the floor.

The Administrator smoothed a finger over one bushy eyebrow. "Very well. You and Dayla wait in the hall until I call you."

They left, and the Administrator focused his attention on me.

"You must be Tria Contry. Welcome to South Back to Basics School. It may be a bit difficult for you at first, but your mother said you couldn't wait until next semester. She said it was imperative that you come to us immediately."

His eyes traveled over me, and I became conscious of my sand-spattered clothes, my gritty skin, and the way my sweaty hair was falling out of its clip. I brushed at the red dust covering my shirt, but I didn't really care what I looked like. "I need a holo projector right away!"

The Administrator crossed his freckled arms and leaned back in his chair. "At South Back to Basics School we deal with reality, with real life that you can't turn on and off. We're returning to a simpler, basic life." He smiled. "In other words, no holograms, no projectors."

No holograms? No projectors? I grabbed the front of his desk and held on tight. "But you must have a projector. Everyone has one. My mom's in danger—"

"Please don't try those kinds of stories on me." His bushy eyebrows pinched together. "I've heard it all before. Besides, I just spoke with your mother yesterday."

"But—"

"And that reminds me: Please turn over any technological instruments you may have—pocket communicators, personal holo projectors, mini-vids, that kind of thing." He held out his upturned hand and wiggled his fingers, waiting for me to put my devices in it. "We don't permit our students to use such instruments, and there will be a severe penalty if you hide anything."

I put my hands on my hips. "If I had a personal projector, I wouldn't be begging you for one."

"Incoming call. Incoming call."

I spotted the communications screen in the back corner of his office. "I thought you didn't like technology," I accused. Not that it was very technological. It was just an old-fashioned flat screen, not a holo call machine.

The Administrator's forehead creased. "It's just for emergencies. Answer call."

A rough-bearded man in a wrinkled flight suit leered unpleasantly at us from the screen. "I have a message for Tria Contry," he said.

The Administrator glanced at me and back to the man. "Who are you? What is the emergency?"

"You may call me Captain." He must have seen the way the Administrator looked at me when he mentioned my name. As the Captain turned to face me, I could see the ring in his nose glimmer. "Tria, my dear niece," he began.

Niece? Who was this scuzzy-looking man?

"Your mother is visiting me, and we would like you to join us."

I didn't like the sound of that. "Where's my mom? Is she okay?"

The Administrator spoke at the same time. "This doesn't sound like an emergency. How did you get this number?"

The Captain shoved a hand into his pocket and brought out something small and sparkly. "Your mother is fine. For now." He dangled a gold filigree earring with little glass balls.

"If she's fine, then there's no emergency," the Administrator said, tapping his fingers impatiently on the desk. "And I don't believe you're on Tria's list of authorized visitors." He swiveled to face his info screen and started muttering at it.

Prickles of unease crawled over my skin. "What do you mean, she's fine for now?"

"We'll be arriving in town tomorrow at noon. Come then, and bring it with you."

It? Did he mean Star? Surely no one would refer to Star as "it."

The Captain squeezed Mom's earring tightly in his hand.

"You're not on the list!" The Administrator

swiveled back to face the Captain. "I'm going to terminate this unauthorized call right now."

Even through the Administrator's voice, I heard the crunch of the blown glass balls breaking. The Captain opened his hand, showing the delicate balls and gold filigree crushed and twisted in his callused palm.

"Or else," he said. Then he disconnected.

chapter five

"These new technologies never work right," the Administrator grumbled. "He shouldn't have been able to get this number."

My mind was spinning. Who was that man?

"I'm sorry, Tria." The Administrator shook his head. "Sometimes it's difficult for relatives to understand. Constant access to technology ruins everything we're trying to teach here. We've had to increase security to keep unauthorized people away and"—he gave me a sharp glance—"to keep students from sneaking to town for techno-thrills. Your uncle will have to wait for proper authorization before you can visit him."

I snapped out of my daze. "He's not my uncle! You heard him—he's got my mother and he'll hurt her unless I bring him whatever it is he wants. You have to help me."

"Don't be melodramatic," he said, then softened his brisk tone. "I'll make a deal with you. If you'll agree to settle down and stop telling tales, I'll put a call through to your mother so you can see she's all right."

"Deal!" I said quickly.

He nodded and whispered to his info screen. The communications screen produced several quick beeps.

"No answer. We'll try again later."

"Try again now!"

"Later." He picked up a floppy white hat from his desk. "Here's your official Back to Basics School hat. Don't go outside without it. You'll find a uniform in your pod. It is made of natural fibers that will protect you from the sun and keep you cool." He raised his voice. "Dayla! Brash! Show Ms. Contry to her pod so she can clean up for lunch."

He handed me the floppy hat and I put it on, thinking furiously. He hadn't kept his side of the deal, so I didn't have to keep mine. There was nothing at Back to Basics School for me. No holo projector and no help for my mother. Maybe someone in town would help me.

I darted out of the office and hurtled Outside.

"Door open!" I yelled as I ran toward the wall. But it stayed solidly closed. I slid to a stop in a cloud of red sandy dust. "Door open! Open!"

Then I saw the red keypad lights on the wall.

"It's not voice activated, Fluff Brain," Dayla said behind me. "We entered a code to let you in. And," she went on, dashing my hopes, "the code changes every five minutes. So I can't open it and get rid of you."

I stared at the door. If I had my WonderTool, I'd make the wall open. But the mover was still packing it up. Along with the rest of my life.

"Come along," Brash said softly.

I looked wildly around. I had to get out! But the wall was solid. Or was it? Maybe it was a hologram.

I pounded on it. Solid. Well then, I would climb it. I leaped at the wall, scrabbling for a handhold. The wall was smooth as glass. I slid back down and fell to the ground. "Ow!" The sand wasn't as soft a landing as my sofa back home. I rubbed my scraped hands and hauled myself painfully to my feet.

Star, help! I cried silently. But she couldn't. I was on my own.

"No one can cross the wall," Brash said. "There are energy barriers on top."

"Find your own pod, Fluff Brain," Dayla said. "I'm going to lunch." I heard her footsteps crunching away across the sand.

If I couldn't get through the wall, then I needed to go back inside. I couldn't think out here. I looked desperately at Brash. "Help me," I croaked.

He held out my dust-covered hat. "You need food."

I shoved the hat back on my head and stumbled after Brash. I didn't want to eat or wash up. I just wanted to find a holo projector and ask Star what "it" was so we could rescue Mom. But I didn't know what else to do.

Brash led me to a building. Rich, spicy smells drifted out, making my stomach rumble. Dayla had walked in the door ahead of us as if nothing were wrong, but I stopped and eyed it uneasily.

The building was roaring.

Brash spoke behind me. "This is the Food Hall. Your pod is there." Brash pointed past all the nearby buildings to a low mound, hazy in the distance.

The backs of my legs were aching and my forehead was throbbing like when I wore my AR headband for too long. I couldn't walk all the way Outside without rest and water. Unless . . . "Is there an underground walkway?"

Brash shook his head.

My shoulders slumped. The AlmostReality terrain from DugganV had an underground walkway between its monuments. Why couldn't they have something like that here? I rubbed my eyes and reluctantly turned back to the noisy building. Inside was always better than Outside. Even if the hall was roaring.

"I don't like this," I said, like it would make a difference. "I want to go home. I don't want to be Outside. I don't like germy real people." Something shrieked over the roaring, and I edged away from the door. "And I especially don't like animals."

A look of sadness crossed Brash's face. "No animals are allowed."

I've had all the biopreventives, I reminded myself. And if Dayla could go in there, so could I. I let Brash go through the door first, steeling myself for whatever waited inside.

The press of sound overwhelmed me. There were kids everywhere. They sat at long tables crowded with plates of steaming vegetables and crusty breads. They were eating and yelling at the same time. A mob pushed and shoved at the far end of the room. Kids swarmed in all directions.

"I want out," I said, backing up. But someone pushed me aside and sidled up to Brash.

"Want to see my coral spud?" The kid held up his

cupped hands, and a triangular orange snout poked between his fingers.

A spud! I shrieked and turned to run. But I couldn't get through the crowd to the door. I pushed and shoved, bouncing off solid bodies, being pushed in return, until I ended up against a wall. I sank to the floor and buried my head in my arms, gulping for air. Any minute I knew I'd feel tiny lizard teeth sink like needles into my skin. Or perhaps there was a stinger in the spud's tail that would slap me with one burning, lethal jolt. I tried to make myself as small and still as possible.

Time passed. Eventually I lifted my head. I'd blocked out the noise while I cowered, waiting for that coral spud to bite me. But the mass of kids was just the same, the thunder of voices was just the same. No one had been bitten.

An Omegan slither spud had bitten Dad. Maybe a coral spud was different?

My hair clip had fallen out. I picked it up with trembling fingers and clipped my tangled hair into a bunch again. Near me I heard the sound of a familiar name and tuned in.

"Dayla says she told the new girl to stay away," a girl said. "Poor thing. What's wrong with Dayla anyway?"

Another girl giggled, high and shrill. "Didn't you hear? She keeps messing up her father's diplomatic missions with her big mouth and bad manners. She even told the Cruxor ambassador his food was stinky. They say her mother left because she couldn't stand Dayla anymore!" The two girls exploded into laughter, and the rest of their discussion was lost in the babble.

"Tria?" Brash came up beside me.

I took a shaky breath. "Let's get out of here."

He turned and threaded his way through the crowd. I wished I dared to catch hold of his T-shirt. Instead I walked as close to him as I could. As soon as we stepped Outside, the noise level lessened, and for the first time in my life I was relieved not to be inside.

Brash reached into the pouch hanging from his survival belt. "Food. Water." He held out a sandwich and a bottle. Gratefully I took them and squatted against the wall of the building in a sliver of shade. The water was cold and the peanut butter sandwich was delicious.

"Thanks." I took a final swallow from the water bottle and scanned Brash. "Are you okay? The spud didn't bite you?"

"Shhh!" Brash shoved the empty bottle into his

pouch and looked around furtively. "Pets are not being allowed."

"Pets?" I squeaked. "That horrifying creature?" I felt queasy even thinking about it.

He frowned at me from under his hat. "Coral spuds are not horrifying."

Without another word he led me to the Residence Hall and found my pod.

"Open," Brash said, and it did.

I was relieved to have my own place again. I hoped it was going to be safe.

chapter six

"**Aren't they** locked?" I asked, peeking through the door of my pod. No one else was in there. "Or at least personalized to my voice?"

"No. I will return and take you to class." Brash nodded at me and left.

Tiny and white, the pod was completely empty except for a sleep shelf with two light green T-shirts and matching pants lying on it. A faint lemon smell hung in the air.

None of my things were here. I couldn't go to town unless I had my WonderTool to open that gate. Em should have delivered everything by now. Maybe she'd been intercepted by the phony mover with the stunner. Maybe my stuff was never coming. Maybe Em was . . .

I sank onto the sleep shelf. Zell wouldn't really

shoot anyone, would she? Especially Em, who didn't know anything about Star or a secret message.

And what about Mom? I shook off the thought. She was all right. She had to be.

I pulled off my shoes, fished out Star's disk, and held it tight.

"Star, I can't do this. It's too scary and dangerous." I stared at the shiny silver disk for a moment. Then I squared my shoulders, scooped up the uniform, and headed for the shower. Because it didn't matter if I said I couldn't do it. I had to.

Warm water pelted down on me, washing away the sand and sweat. I discovered black and blue marks and scraped-up skin, probably from falling off the barrier wall. I never got this banged up in AlmostReality. I clutched Star's disk in one hand the whole time I showered. Thank goodness she was waterproof. I wanted her close beside me in this strange place.

Once I was dressed, I waited for Brash in the corridor, my clean hair pulled neatly into its clip and Star stuffed safely in my shoe. I felt stronger and calmer, back in control again.

As soon as I saw Brash, he ducked his head, so I had to talk to the top of his floppy hat. I'd lost my own hat somewhere, but I didn't care.

"My things aren't here, Brash. I have to make a call to the movers and find out what happened."

Brash shook his head, still staring at the floor. "Calls are not allowed. We will check storage. After class." He shot a quick look at me. "You need your hat to stop sunstroke."

"Never mind that. And I'm not going to class. Show me storage now."

"Class is now." He pulled off his hat and handed it to me. For the first time I saw that his heavy straight hair was blunt cut across his forehead. "Take it."

For a nanosecond I considered exploring on my own. Going Outside and searching buildings. Buildings where coral spuds might live. I could do it. I could do anything for Mom and Star. Then an image of that repulsive orange head flashed through my mind. I took the hat Brash was still holding and shoved it over my damp hair.

Brash led the way to another mound building. We stepped into a classroom, and a skinny woman with big teeth smiled at us.

"Welcome, Tria. I'm your teacher, Ms. Linden."

Brash slid into a seat and I stood there feeling awkward, while dozens of eyes stared at me.

"Class, this is Tria Contry, who is joining us from

45

Dulles City. Please make her feel welcome. Tria, sit at that desk beside Dayla."

Dayla stuck out her foot, but I stepped over it and sat down quickly.

At least the classroom was quieter than the Food Hall. But a real-time human teacher and living, breathing, germy kids were right here with me. And maybe some animals, too. I ducked my head and slid low in my seat.

"Now, class," Ms. Linden said. "Is everyone ready for ArborQuest? Tria, you'll be on Dayla and Brash's team. I hope you're feeling like a team already, since they met your scooter and showed you around."

Dayla snorted and muttered something.

"Dayla, one of your achievement challenges is to get along with your teammates," the teacher said sharply. "Is that clear?"

Dayla gave a reluctant nod, and Ms. Linden continued. "Now, as you know, the first team to return with a bilo leaf and a hyperweed report wins."

"Don't you want a hyperweed leaf, too?" a girl with a high, shrill voice asked.

I glanced up, recognizing the voice. She was the one who'd been talking about Dayla in the Food Hall.

"After all," she went on with a toss of her head, "some people might cheat." She looked meaningfully at Dayla.

"I don't cheat, Nanohead," Dayla shouted, jumping up.

"Sit down, Dayla. Be quiet, Meta." Ms. Linden made little patting motions in the air.

Dayla ignored her. "I'll win this ArborQuest so fast you'll still be sitting at the starting line when I get back."

"Sit, Dayla." Ms. Linden's pats were getting more agitated.

Meta shrugged. "Your rich daddy still won't want you at home. And your mother ran so far away from you that nobody even knows where she is."

Some of the kids laughed, and Dayla turned red. I watched her with interest. Was she going to explode into red and krylar yellow pieces?

Ms. Linden stopped patting the air. "Sit down, Dayla. Meta, I'll speak with you after class." Her voice was so cold and firm that even Dayla wilted. "We do not require a hyperweed leaf, Meta, because not all of the bilo trees have been invaded. So not all of you will find hyperweeds. We do require, though, that you use map-reading skills, basic flora identification, and"—she paused significantly—"teamwork."

She talked on, but now that I knew no one was going to explode, my mind wandered to my own problems. I tried to plan, but felt like I was trying to do one of those logic puzzles I could never solve. Where could I get a holo projector? How was I going to unlock the gate? Where was my WonderTool? How would I get across the miles of scrubby desert?

Star was a whiz at logic puzzles and always helped me work them out. How was I going to solve this one without her?

Would the Administrator consider my WonderTool a technological instrument? Probably. It was a good thing I hadn't had it in my pocket when I met him, or he would have confiscated it. Suddenly my eyes widened. Maybe he had already confiscated someone's personal projector. And maybe he had it locked up in his office. All I had to do was get my WonderTool, wait until the Administrator was gone, and visit his office. Simple. *I'll be seeing you soon, Star,* I said silently. And after Star told me what "it" was, we'd figure out how to get to town. I leaned back in my seat, a grin spreading over my face.

After an eternity, class ended. I stood up, trying to keep my eyes on Brash. Everyone was running, bumping, yelling.

I have to be strong for Mom, I reminded myself. Dayla had left, thank goodness. But Brash was gone, too. I walked to the door and gingerly stepped Outside. Hot air wrapped around me, and the blinding light made me pull Brash's hat down over my eyes. I walked carefully, feeling the sand move under my feet. I hadn't noticed the way the sand felt before. It was interesting the way all those little bits could roll around and still be solid enough to support you. When I looked down, I saw red dust puffing up with every step.

"You! New Girl! Freeze!"

Someone jumped in front of me. I squinted from under the hat. Krylar yellow hair. It was Dayla.

She put her hands on her hips. "You'll never keep up with us tomorrow. We'll leave you far behind. You'll be all alone, stranded and lost."

All alone? Lost? I already was.

"My father's rich, you know." Dayla smirked. "He bought me my own robo horse. Brash's grant committee bought one for him. But you'll have to use a broken-down school horse."

Relief and excitement bubbled up in me. "I have the best robo horse on the planet. Thanks for reminding me."

I hoped Em had packed and delivered Mom's old robo horse with the rest of my stuff. I could ride it to town after I got the holo projector and heard Star's message. My plans were coming together.

"*Nothing* is better than my robo horse," Dayla shouted. "He's top of the line."

"Tria!"

I spotted Brash beside a thorny bush, waving at me. "Storage is over here."

"Let's see this wonderful robo horse of yours," Dayla said, sprinting past. "I bet it's nothing more than a decrepit bag of bolts."

I caught up with Brash and Dayla in the cool dimness of the storage entrance. Dayla stood in front of a directory board, murmuring and punching lights.

"West 55," she announced. "Hey! No one's certified your stuff yet."

"Then we will leave." Brash turned to me. "You cannot have your boxes until a teacher checks that they are"—he said the words carefully—"technologically appropriate."

I shook my head. "I need my horse now. I can't wait for some teacher."

"You must. Come along."

"Hold it," ordered Dayla. "You're not going anywhere. I want to see this oh-so-wonderful robo horse." Her fingers flew over the board. "There! Mr. Prender just certified your stuff."

"He did?" Brash looked around, puzzled.

"Grow up, Farm Boy. I used his code." Dayla swaggered down the corridor.

I stood for a moment, stunned. Dayla had helped me! She was just being obnoxious, but still . . .

"Thanks!" I called, hurrying after her.

"I will be glad to have you on my team," Brash said, falling into step with me. "I don't want to be alone with Dayla for a whole day."

I laughed before I remembered that I wouldn't be on Brash's team. I planned to be out of here first thing next morning. Guilt washed over me. Brash had shared his food and water and showed me my pod. He was almost as good as a holo friend. But Mom and Star came first.

Dayla was pacing impatiently in front of West 55. "I bet the robo horse is in that big box," she said, pointing through the wire mesh. "Well, go on, show me."

I bit my lip. My horse didn't need a big box anymore. Not since I'd used my WonderTool to take it apart a few months ago. I'd never gotten around to putting it back together.

Dayla hooted. "Fluff Brain! Don't you even know how to access storage?" She went on in a baby voice: "First you ask for Directory."

Was the whole thing voice activated? "Directory."

"Read me first."

"Okay. Read."

"Hello, Tria. I hope you enjoyed your scooter ride and arrived safely."

At first I couldn't identify the speaker. But as she continued, I had it. Em the mover!

"I had a bit of trouble. Two goons tried to hijack my load. They were no match for me, though, and the doctors say my arm is just scorched." Em's voice crackled with satisfaction. "I reported them to the Planetary Guards. Good luck with your new life. This is Em, signing off."

My aching legs folded under me, and I sat down hard on the floor. Her arm was scorched! Someone had shot at her. And they'd used a more powerful weapon than a stunner.

Brash and Dayla were staring at me. Brash with concern, Dayla with contempt. "What's your problem, Fluff Brain? Nothing was stolen, nobody was really hurt."

I ignored her. I had to get to Mom fast, before she got hurt, too. "Directory, WonderTool."

"*Boxes 23 through 27.*" Five boxes for a Wonder-Tool? With a grinding and clanking, the boxes started to move. They seemed to be on some kind of conveyor belt. What a weird mix of technologies. Five boxes slid down and rocked on the floor.

Brash stood on his toes to read the labels. " 'Small Items. Living Room.' "

Oh, great. I'd have to go through all these boxes. "Robo horse body," I continued.

"Body? What do you mean, body?" Dayla asked.

I didn't look at her as Box 17 slipped onto the floor.

"This is it?" Dayla had the beginnings of a smile on her face. "*This* little box is your wonderful robo horse?"

I needed to be sure it was the right box. So I didn't stop Dayla when she ripped it open and pawed through the packing material. Then she laughed and tipped the box over.

The limp golden brown robo horse body fell out, along with a shower of packing material. Its

53

legs were tucked up under its belly and its long neck lay in a graceful curve along the floor. The robo horse's dark gold tail spread over its body like a blanket. It looked like it was asleep. Or dead.

chapter seven

Dayla's laughter echoed through the storage room. "Don't even bother to show up tomorrow, Fluff Brain. You are going nowhere on this!"

Dayla nudged the robo horse with her toe and laughed again. Suddenly she squinted at the packing material, leaned over, and pulled a fist-sized pink rock out of the pile of soft packing.

"What's this?" she asked, holding it up to the light. "Pretty." She stuffed it in her pocket and walked away, chuckling to herself.

"That is not yours!" said Brash, starting after her.

"Never mind. It's just a rock." I sighed, looking at all the boxes I was going to have to sort through. "It's not important."

Brash helped me stuff the robo horse back into its

box. Then we found an old-fashioned wheeled transport and rolled the six boxes back to my pod.

My tiny pod was even tinier with the boxes in it.
Brash opened them with a tool from his belt. I gave each
"Small Items. Living Room" box a shove and tipped the
contents onto the floor. Boards, circuits, kernels, hard
shells, and cubes cascaded out. Pieces of my experiments were here, but where was my WonderTool?

Brash picked up a circuit cube and put it down
again. "What are these things?" he asked, spreading
his hands wide to indicate the littered floor.

I pawed through a pile of segmented cylinders.
"The components of my Home Tutor, my Fly-by-
night, the residence cleaner, the atmosphere controller . . ." Brash's face was blank. "You know, toys
and appliances. Except the pieces of Mr. Willoughby,
my Home Tutor. He's a computerized intelligence. I
like to take things apart and see how they work."

The big Olympian vase tumbled out of Box 24. I
barely caught it before it hit the ground. "Whew!
Mom would have been upset if I'd broken that." I
carefully stood it to one side.

"You will fix your horse for ArborQuest now?"
Brash asked.

I was blinking back tears, thinking about Mom.

"ArborQuest?" I repeated shrilly. "My mom's in danger and you're talking to me about ArborQuest?"

"Danger?" Brash's voice was puzzled. "I did not know your mother was in danger."

"Of course you didn't. The Administrator didn't believe a word I said." I sat back on my heels. Looking at Brash's bent head, I realized I was still wearing his hat. I pulled it off and tossed it to him. He looked up just in time to catch it.

"Tell me," he said, twisting the hat in his hands.

I scooped up a handful of small components and stuffed them back into the Olympian vase. I was sure Brash wouldn't be able to stop me from leaving even if he wanted to. So I kept sorting, scooping, and stuffing as I talked.

"My mom has been kidnapped and I have to get to town by noon tomorrow or they'll hurt her. And I had to turn off my best friend." I sniffed and wiped my nose with my fist. Talking about it made it more real somehow. "Star has important information that will save Mom. First I need to find my—there it is!" I pounced on a pile of cell flats and pulled my WonderTool out from under them. It seemed fine, so I buttoned it quickly into my pocket, where it couldn't get lost again. "Now I just need to get a holo projector."

Brash opened his mouth.

"I know," I said, holding up my hand to stop him. "No projectors allowed. But what if the Administrator confiscated one? I'm going to look around his office tonight."

Brash nodded. "Yes, he confiscated it."

My hands were full of more pieces to stuff into the vase, but the pieces never got there. My fingers lost their strength, and everything dropped to the floor.

"You mean there really is one?"

"When I first came, I had no belief in holograms." Brash turned red as I stared in disbelief at him. "So Dayla showed me with her projector. She thought to make me look stupid. And she did."

I let out the breath I hadn't known I'd been holding. "And the Administrator caught her and took the projector away?"

"Yes."

Excitement and relief bubbled up in me. Soon I would see Star! "Tonight I'll get that projector."

Brash looked apprehensive. "Are you certain this is a good plan?"

I nodded and jumped up. "I'd better start on the robo horse so I can leave right after that."

Various components littered the floor around the

golden chestnut robo horse body. It would be tricky sorting out which ones went with the horse, but toys and appliances had a lot of interchangeable parts. The important thing would be the brain boards. I searched around, picking up likely looking pieces and piling them near the horse. "Brash, when will the Administrator leave his office?"

Brash shook his head. "This is a plan with problems."

"What problems?" I sat down beside the robo horse and turned on my WonderTool.

"Everyone will be going for the meal soon." Brash moved over to sit on the sleep shelf. "But after that security guards start patrolling. They have weapons."

"No school would have real guards with real weapons." I leaned over and tugged the locomotor closer. "I bet they're holograms. Have you checked?"

I started shoving circuit cubes and chip strips into the robo horse as fast as I could. *Zap!* I fused a connection. *Zap!* Another piece in place. This robo horse was going to be ready tonight. *Zap!* I was getting that holo projector and I was leaving. *Zap!*

Brash's pale moon face grew even paler. "No, I have not checked. They have *weapons.*"

"I forgot. You're not used to holograms." My hands stopped. "I wonder how many other kids aren't used to technology? That's probably what they're counting on. Well, I know different. But I'll be back before the guards come on duty anyway. I'll pretend to go to the Food Hall but slip away to the office instead."

Brash slid off the sleep shelf and scooped up a handful of components. "I will help you with this robo horse. They are not as nice as furbeasts, though. Their coats are too smooth. But they are useful animals."

"They're not animals." I grimaced at the thought. "They just look like them."

"Yes. But Tria, the guards . . ."

I plucked a connector from Brash's hand. *Zap!* My mind was made up. *Zap!* And I didn't want to hear Brash's arguments. *Zap!* Star was the only person who could ever change my mind once it was made up. *Zap!* And Star wasn't saying anything. *Zap! Zap!*

I snatched pieces from the floor and shoved them into the robo horse.

"Tria—"

Zap! "It's harder to put this in than it was to take it out," I said, trying to jiggle a gray pink wedge into place. Brash held it down while I zapped some extra connections around it.

Dinner was only half an hour away when I finally put down my WonderTool.

"Help me stand it up, Brash."

Together we heaved the robo horse to its feet.

"It feels like an animal now, does it not?" Brash smoothed the plush golden hairs of the horse's coat. "Your horse has better muscling than mine. And his bone structure is much finer."

"It doesn't have muscles and bones," I explained. "It's a technological creation." I felt a thrill of excitement as I climbed onto the sleep shelf and reached between the robo horse's fuzzy ears.

"Now for the big test!" I flipped the On switch.

At first nothing happened. Then the long, silky tail swished. The solid hooves moved slowly. The ears swiveled and the robo horse opened its large brown eyes and turned to look at me. It had a white star on its forehead and a thin white stripe down its nose. It really was rather pretty.

"You did it!" Brash jumped up and down in excitement.

I leaped off the sleep shelf. "I've never put anything so big back together before!"

The robo horse opened its mouth. "Tria, have you completed your assignment?"

I sat down hard.

Brash's jaw dropped. "Robo horses do not talk."

"Of course robo horses don't talk," said the robo horse in a smooth, deep voice. "Tria, your last assignment was a geopolitical holo map. Is it finished?" The robo horse lowered its fine-boned head and looked me in the eye.

I stared back. "Mr. Willoughby!"

chapter eight

Oh no! What had I done?

"I must have mixed up some of the circuits," I mumbled, even more shocked than I was the time I'd accidentally made the residence cleaner blow dust all over the pod. "Or maybe the chips got scrambled when I dumped them out of the box."

"I suppose that means you don't have the holo map," the robo horse said, pursing his lips. "You must learn to complete your projects, Tria. Where's Star? And perhaps you'll introduce me to your friend?"

I gulped. "Star's here." I rubbed my foot over her disk. "I'd like you to meet Brash. He's real. Brash, this is my, um, Home Tutor."

"My name is Mr. Willoughby." The robo horse nodded politely to Brash.

"I am most pleased to meet you, sir." Brash looked earnestly into Mr. Willoughby's soft liquid eyes.

"Do you know," the robo horse said, moving his head slowly to the left, "I believe you've changed my visual pickups. The audio seems different, too," he said, wiggling his ears around.

"Mr. Willoughby, I have something to tell you." This wasn't going to be easy. I took a deep breath and said it fast, "You're a robo horse."

"Excuse me?" the robo horse said, his mane flying out as he turned toward me again.

I closed my eyes so I wouldn't have to see his face and rushed through the words a second time. "You'rearobohorse."

"I. Am. A. Robo. Horse?" the robo horse said very slowly, as if examining each word for meaning.

"Yes." I peeked at him and saw his head jerk up and his eyes widen until the whites showed. I hurried on. "I needed a robo horse, you see, so I put you together. But I didn't mean to put *you* together. I mean you, the Home Tutor. I meant to put the robo horse together. And, well, I guess things got a little mixed up."

"A little mixed up," the robo horse repeated.

Why hadn't I paid more attention to what I was

doing? "I'm really sorry, but I'm glad you're my robo horse now," I whispered. He blinked and lowered his head a bit. "He makes a wonderful robo horse, doesn't he, Brash?"

Brash gave a quick nod. "You are being most magnificent and handsome."

"Absolutely!" I agreed, looking with satisfaction at Mr. Willoughby's shiny chestnut coat. The dark gold of his mane set off the lighter gold of his coat to perfection.

Brash stepped closer to Mr. Willoughby and held out his hand. "I have not seen another horse as fine as you."

The robo horse stretched out his neck and sniffed Brash's hand. Then he drew back quickly, looking surprised at himself.

"This was my mother's horse," I reminded Mr. Willoughby. "She always loved it. And way back when she was a kid, they made a much higher-quality robo horse. You're top of the line, Mr. Willoughby."

Mr. Willoughby flared his nostrils.

Brash moved closer. "You are the best robo horse ever! If you helped, I know we would win ArborQuest. That is a contest for our science class."

"The best robo horse ever," the robo horse repeated

flatly. Then the muscles in his neck relaxed, and his eyes glinted with interest. He cocked his head. "Science class?"

"Oh," I said, "you don't know about that. Well, you see, after I took you apart . . ."

Mr. Willoughby laid his ears back. "You took me apart?"

"Yes." I twisted my fingers together nervously. Maybe I'd better not confuse him with kidnapping and mysterious messages yet. "Well, after that Mom sent me to Back to Basics School. You know, with real-time human teachers and real-time human kids."

Mr. Willoughby looked down his nose at me. "Back to Basics School. For those students who can't or won't work on their own with their Home Tutor."

I stared at my hands. "Yes. That's where we are right now."

Mr. Willoughby's eyes opened wide in astonishment. "You went Outside, Tria? With germs and people?"

I felt a little surge of pride. "Yes. Yes, I did."

"I see." The robo horse looked thoughtful. "And you want me to assist you and other students with a school assignment."

Before I could say anything, Brash shouted, "Yes!"

His eyes were sparkling, and his moon face was split by a happy smile. I stared at him in surprise.

"I will be the first Mobile Away-From-Home Tutor," said the robo horse with a faraway look. "I will revolutionize the educational system. I must keep extensive notes and submit articles to all of the scholarly journals. Everyone will know my name and quote me."

"So you will be coming with us?" Brash asked, hesitantly stroking Mr. Willoughby's shoulder.

Mr. Willoughby gave a brisk nod. "That's what I'm here for." He lowered his head to sniff the floor matting. When he raised his head, his muzzle was covered with red sand. Brash and I must have tracked it in from Outside.

I started giggling.

"You are in need of grooming, Mr. Willoughby," Brash said. "Your coat is covered with dust, your mane and tail are tangled, and your mouth . . . Permit me." Brash wiped off the red sand mustache with his sleeve and then unhooked something from his survival belt. "I can comb"—he held up a comb, and I shook my head in astonishment—"and groom with a damp cloth."

Mr. Willoughby wiggled his lips where Brash had

wiped them. "I am rather dirty. Please proceed. Now, what is the learning goal for this ArborQuest?"

I remembered. "We're supposed to find a bilo leaf and report on some kind of weed. But Mr. Willoughby, there's more I have to tell you."

Swiftly I explained to him about Mom and Star. "And the phony movers tried to get Star from me and they fired on Em the mover. And then when I got here the Captain called and said Mom was visiting him. But then he crushed her earring and said she'd be okay only if I brought him 'it' by noon tomorrow." I paused to take a breath.

"Oh my," murmured Mr. Willoughby, eyes wide. Brash had stopped combing and was watching me intently as I added these new details.

"So I really need Star back to hear her message." *And because I miss her,* I added to myself. "I hope she knows what 'it' is. I'm going to visit the Administrator's office during the next meal and use a confiscated projector. Brash says there are guards, but I'll be back before they come on duty. Besides, they're probably holograms."

Mr. Willoughby swished his tail. "Tria, I would surmise that those guards are real."

"They're holograms," I said stubbornly. Then I

changed the subject. "I need some maps of the area."
I realized I didn't even know which town was nearest. Panic flooded through me. How was I going to do this?

"Yes, of course. And Brash, you will need maps of the local flora so you can locate a bilo tree. Let me see." He tilted his head, and I could almost see him thinking. "I'm not sure what my capabilities are in this new body. Yes, I can access maps. Can I—no, I can't project them and I don't seem to have any screens." Brash, who was combing Mr. Willoughby's mane again, got tugged along when Mr. Willoughby swung his long neck around to look at his new body.

"I need maps!" I complained. "How can I get anywhere without maps?"

Brash gave me a perplexed look. "But you know all about technology." He put down his comb and stepped over the pieces on the floor until he reached the wall by the door. I saw the outline then. I hadn't imagined anyone still used flatcomps, an ancient form of map.

"What a primitive—" I started to say while Brash ran his hands over the wall, bringing the flatcomp to life.

"It is most marvelous," he said, beaming at me.

Suddenly I realized he was *looking* at me. He hadn't ducked his head or hid his face since we'd switched Mr. Willoughby on.

I nodded. "Most marvelous."

Brash went back to grooming Mr. Willoughby. "We do not have technologies on my farm," he confided to the robo horse. "I did not see any people except my parents and brother until I came here. My parents schooled us every night."

He'd never seen other people? Not even on holo vids? Well, that explained a lot. What must Brash's life have been like? Never seeing anyone or anything new, not even on a vid. No wonder he made friends with furbeasts.

Brash and Mr. Willoughby continued to chatter together while I studied the terrain between the only town nearby and the school. Most of it was colored orange. I found the map key. Orange meant unstable terrain. Exactly what did that mean? I'd have to ask Mr. Willoughby.

Brash handed me a damp towel when I walked over. "You can clean that side and do not be forgetting his face."

Mr. Willoughby's mane and tail were smooth and tangle-free. Brash was carefully going over the coat with circular motions.

I covered my hand with the towel and moved to Mr. Willoughby's other side. Tentatively I touched his neck. It was different now that the robo horse was activated. Mr. Willoughby was real and he was . . . an animal. Logically I knew better, but my mind went blank and my body had a hard time believing it. My fingers were trembling as I rubbed the cloth against the hairs of his coat.

Just then a clanging noise reverberated through the room.

"It is the bell for the meal." Brash stood up and looked uncertainly at me. "Are you coming?"

"I'll walk out with you." I picked up my Wonder-Tool from the floor and buttoned it into my pocket.

"You will have less than one hour. The guards are patrolling when we are returning to our pods. You must return by then," he added with unusual firmness.

Brash was too naïve about those holo guards. "I'll be fine. Mr. Willoughby, I wish you could come with me." I knew I would feel so much safer with him by my side. "But I guess you'd better stay here. See you later."

Mr. Willoughby crunched his way across the cluttered floor and stopped in front of the door. "Tria, you can't do this. It's not safe."

I stalked over to him and pushed his wide hindquarters. "Move over."

He lowered his head and stared into my eyes. "What about the germs and the insects and the—"

I felt sick, but I clenched my fists. "You and Mom always said Chiron is safe. And I have to get Star back and rescue Mom."

Mr. Willoughby heaved a big sigh and clattered out of my way, mashing components with each step. "If only you'd apply yourself to your studies with that much determination. Be careful."

chapter nine

Brash waved good-bye to Mr. Willoughby. Things looked and felt different as we stepped out of the building. Was Outside always changing? The air was cool against my face, though the sun's rays were still hot on my back. The sun was setting in coral spud colors across the sky. I paused. At home I could set the pod's lights to Sunset, but I'd never seen colors such as these, filling my eyes and stretching to the horizon.

With a start, I remembered that I had to hurry. Time was running out.

As others headed for the Dining Hall, I veered off toward the Administrator's office, away from the crowd.

Brash stayed with me. "I will come along, too."

I stopped. "But you think the guards are real."

"Even so. I want to help."

Brash didn't know my mom or Star. But he was willing to risk running into the guards and their weapons to help me. I didn't want to go across the sand and into that office by myself, but slowly I shook my head. "No. Thanks, but I'll be faster alone."

Brash bowed his head. When he looked up again, he echoed Mr. Willoughby. "Be careful," he said. "And be fast."

"I will." The sun cast my shadow behind me, long and dark. I would hurry. Not because of the guards, but because of the coming darkness. Animals came out when the sun went down. I wanted to be safely inside by then.

Luckily, I didn't need my WonderTool to get into the building. I hurried to the Administrator's office and whispered, "Open."

When nothing happened I pulled out my Wonder-Tool and got to work. A minute later the door popped open, and I darted inside. The office had no windows and was lit only by nightglows.

My eyes fell on the communication screen. I could call for help! I'd always wanted to say "Emergency 511" and get connected to the Planetary Guards.

"Call connect! Emergency 511!"

"Authorization code?"

Who would have thought the Administrator would know enough to install a security barrier? "Um, B2B?"

"Authorization denied."

There wasn't time to try different codes or break the security barrier with my WonderTool. Frustrated, I tried to guess some likely places for confiscated technologies. The cabinet behind the Administrator's desk opened after I gave it a quick jolt with the WonderTool.

There was a projector on the second shelf! But my heart sank when I got a closer look. It was battered, bent, and chipped. I couldn't use this old thing for Star. I could just make out the faded letters *A Bunny Friend* in flakes of blue paint on the side. I smiled, remembering my Betty Bunny lecturing me about friendship. Those Bunny Friends—like Betty, Lucy the Liar, and Bert the Bully—had been an important part of my childhood. And everyone else's, I guessed. Except Brash's.

I hurriedly searched through the rest of the cabinet. I didn't need a Bunny Friends projector—I needed Dayla's new one! Pocket communicators without power cells, game disks, even a broken WonderTool, but no other projectors. The dilapidated Bunny Friends projector would have to do.

Wiping my sweaty hands on my pants, I slipped off my shoe and tried to slide Star's disk into the single projection slot. The projector was so beaten and bent that I had to jiggle the disk around. Finally, it slid into place. I could hardly wait to see Star again.

And there she was, still in that silly Borgarian outfit, violet hair cascading down the back of her embroidered jacket. She flickered and I gasped, afraid I'd lose her, but she steadied into her old self.

"Star!" I felt like I was going to burst with happiness. If she'd been solid I'd have wrapped my arms around her and hugged her until she couldn't breathe. Had it only been this morning that I'd turned her off?

"Hi, Tria." Star grinned at me, and then her brow wrinkled as she looked around. "Where are we? Is it safe?"

"We're at Back to Basics School and we have to talk fast. Star, it's been awful without you. You can't imagine! Shooting and grabbing and coral spuds! But I saw a bird. A real bird in a real sky!" My voice filled with delighted awe. Star's eyes sparkled, but I remembered we had to hurry. "And Mom is kidnapped and we have to find 'it' and take it to the kidnappers by noon tomorrow to save her. What's 'it,' Star?" I finished breathlessly.

The sparkle died out of Star's eyes. "Your mother was being pursued by thieves who want a device she found on her last dig. She wanted us to take it to a bank and lock it up." She flickered again, and her last words were fuzzy.

"Star!" I shook the projector and she steadied. "Where is it? What does it do? What does it look like?"

"It's hidden . . ." She went thin and transparent. Her voice faded in and out, and I lost some words. ". . . small pink red . . ." She disappeared.

"Star!" I rattled the projector, but it was so old I'd never be able to fix it. Tears streamed down my face as I wiggled Star's disk out and gently slipped it back into my shoe.

I shoved the projector onto the shelf and locked the cabinet. Then, sniffling and wiping my eyes, I snuck back out of the office.

The sun was low on the horizon and the sky was fading to gray. Up ahead, light spilled from the mound-shaped buildings. A cool breeze ruffled my hair, and I shivered. I'd spent longer in there than I'd realized. It was easy to dismiss the thought of the guards but not so easy to banish images of animals creeping through the dusk, especially since I kept hearing faint rustles and skittery noises. *Just the wind,* I told myself.

Star's words nagged at me. "Small pink red." What could it be?

A dark figure—too tall to be a student—crossed in front of one of the buildings. I ducked. Other figures moved about but I managed to avoid them. I rushed inside the Residence Hall, grateful to be safely away from the dark, rustling Outside. My arms were bumpy from the cold. Or maybe from fear. I shouldn't have spent so much time searching for Dayla's projector.

An image flashed through my mind: Dayla bending over to pick up a pink rock. Not "pink red." Pink rock!

Dayla had Mom's device! I glanced around the empty corridors. Brash had pointed out Dayla's pod earlier. I was only two corridors away. I dashed down the hall and around the corner.

Guards! They were dressed in dark gray uniforms that blended into the shadows.

I dashed back around the corner and flattened myself against the wall. There really were guards.

I'd half thought Brash had made them up, just to scare me.

I inched forward. The closest guard was striding away from me, toward two others leaning on a far wall and chatting.

Mentally I saluted their programmer. If a gray arm slipped through a wall, the students might not notice and would still think the guards were real.

I edged around the corner, hoping to sneak up to the next corridor before they noticed me. But I'd forgotten this wasn't my lucky day.

"Hold it," came a voice from behind me.

I turned. It was a guard. And he'd drawn his weapon.

chapter ten

The silver tube in the guard's hand gleamed. Buttons and knobs and raised beading covered it.

"Need any help?" another guard called.

"Everything's under control," the guard in front of me said, fixing me with a stern gaze. His details were very good—the crisp voice, the clear eyes, the dark skin, even the B2B emblem on his uniform pocket looked absolutely real to my expert eye. The whole set of guards must have been quite expensive.

I wasn't going to let them stop me. I dashed forward, dodging to the right. "It's rude to walk through a hologram," Mom had always said.

But the guard dodged with me, so I didn't have a choice. I put my head down and plunged forward into his gray uniformed stomach.

Oof! He was solid! We both went down. I tried to roll away, but he caught my arm and held me tight.

"Let me go!" I pushed at his grabbing, germy fingers.

"New kid, right?" he said, hauling me to my feet. "Bet you thought I was a hologram. Now march."

He held the silver tube in one hand and tugged me along with the other. At the far end of the hallway, the other guards chuckled and started chatting again.

"Which pod is yours?"

I was silent, trying to remember the number of Dayla's pod. Maybe he'd escort me there and go away. But I'd taken too long to answer.

The guard sighed and halted. He slid his weapon back into his belt and held up his pocket communicator, all the while holding on to me.

"Pocket communicators aren't allowed here," I said, hoping to startle him so I could pull away.

He just grinned and spoke into the communicator. "Pod number for a new arrival. East Hall? Thanks."

He led me back to my pod and took out his weapon again. As he raised it, I struggled desperately against his hold.

He held me in place easily. "Open."

My pod opened and he let go. Before I could run back down the hall, he gave me a little shove inside.

"Close. Lock," he said. And as I whirled to face him, he pointed the tube at the outside wall.

Zap!

The door closed. A lock clicked.

"Open!" I shouted. But it didn't.

"Welcome back," Mr. Willoughby said in his deep voice, nudging my shoulder with his nose.

In my head I was still seeing that silver tube and hearing the loud *zap!* Despite everything that had gone wrong, a tingle of envy and awe ran through me.

"Mr. Willoughby, the guards are real, but they don't have weapons. They have Mega-Wonder-Tools!" I stared at the door wistfully. "I've heard of them, but I've only seen them on the webnet. Wish I had one."

Mr. Willoughby tossed his head and gave a loud snort. "You have to be eighteen and have a license."

"I know." I pulled out my WonderTool and then put it away again. I could probably get the pod entry open, but what was the use? The guards would be alert now, and I'd never get past them.

My stomach growled. Was it only this morning when Star had scolded me for putting so much syrup on my pancakes? I wished she were here to scold me now.

"I talked to Star," I told Mr. Willoughby. "But I used an old projector and I only got a few clear words. Just enough to know that Dayla has the device we need."

"Dayla? The girl Brash was telling me about?" Mr. Willoughby blinked. "She must be very unhappy to be so mean to everyone."

"Unhappy?" My voice rose. "She's a menace. And now she's stolen the device." I buried my face in my hands. "And I let her have it. I'm useless, Mr. Willoughby. I can't do anything right."

Mr. Willoughby stretched out his neck and nuzzled my hair. "You did something right. You put me together, didn't you?"

A tear slid down my cheek. "I put you together *wrong*."

Mr. Willoughby spoke softly but firmly. "You put me together *better*. And tomorrow I'll help you persuade Dayla to give back the device."

I brushed away my tears. "You don't know Dayla. But I feel better. Thanks." I leaned over and hugged Mr. Willoughby, wrapping my arms around his soft neck and tangling my fingers in his silky mane.

"You're welcome," mumbled Mr. Willoughby,

with his head low. Then he gave himself a shake and cleared his throat. "I've never been hugged before. It's an extraordinary experience."

I looked down and twisted my fingers together. "Mom is the only other person I've hugged. And Dad, but I don't really remember that."

Mr. Willoughby raised his head. "Tria, I'm not a person."

"Yes, you are!" I hugged him again. "Star is a real person and so are you."

That night was the first time I'd ever gone to bed hungry. I didn't like it. My stomach rumbled and complained as I lay there, thinking about Mom in the hands of that Captain. Was he feeding her? Was she warm enough? Where was she sleeping? I pictured her shivering and hungry, lying on a rocky floor, maybe with racknids and coral spuds crawling and slithering around her. I swore I'd rescue her somehow, even if I didn't find the device. Then my mind switched over to Star and how she flickered and winked out of existence. If our places were reversed, Star would have gotten the device and saved Mom by now. She was a lot more capable than I was. Braver, too.

A soft clanking noise made my blood freeze.

Then I remembered Mr. Willoughby. "What are you doing?" I whispered into the darkness.

The noise stopped. "Sorry. I thought I'd clean up. I was just pushing these pieces into a pile. My nose is getting sandy again, so I'll stop. Go to sleep."

I did. And instead of having nightmares, I dreamed of hot, steaming pancakes soaking in pools of sweet, thick syrup.

A clanging bell woke me.

I sat straight up and stared wildly around. Mr. Willoughby blinked at me, and I remembered where I was. "Bells!" I grumbled, rolling off the sleep shelf. "Why can't they have music?" I winced as I straightened my legs. Every muscle ached from all that walking across the sand yesterday.

I shuffled over to the door. "Open." It didn't. Maybe the guards were gone, though. I could open the pod's entry with my WonderTool and go talk to Dayla. I shuffled back to the sleep shelf, trying to remember if the WonderTool was in my pants pocket.

"Good morning." Mr. Willoughby opened his mouth wide, stuck out his tongue, and wiggled his jaw.

I stared. "Are you yawning?"

He closed his mouth with a snap. A look of

surprised interest crossed his chestnut face. "I believe I was. I don't sleep, of course, but it seemed the proper way to stretch and limber up my components after hours of stillness."

I stretched and yawned, too. "It is the proper way," I agreed.

He clumped over, picked my clothes off the floor with his teeth, and dropped them beside me. "Let's go find Dayla."

I washed and dressed quickly, slipping Star back into my shoe. My empty stomach rumbled.

"Time to break out." I pulled the WonderTool from my pocket and stepped up to the door.

Mr. Willoughby bustled around, rolling cubes and boards into piles with his nose. "Let me know if you need help."

He had another sand mustache, but before I could brush it off, my pod door beeped. And then, *zap!* the door slid open.

A guard stood there, tucking a MegaWonderTool into the pocket of her gray uniform. I hastily hid my own WonderTool behind my back.

"Hello," I said, hoping I sounded innocent. "Thanks for letting me out. I need to stop at a friend's pod before breakfast."

She clasped her arms behind her back and looked

over my shoulder into the pod. She surveyed all the boxes and pieces scattered on the floor and lingered a moment on Mr. Willoughby, who stood unmoving in a corner of the room. "Breakfast is over. It's almost time for class."

"Why didn't you let me out sooner?" I complained.

She stared down at me. "Punishment for last night's episode with the guards. The Administrator's still trying to get in touch with your mother. He asks that you remember your deal."

She pulled something from her pocket and held it out to me. "Nutrition bar. Settle down. Go straight to class." Then she strode away.

I unwrapped the sticky bar and took a huge bite.

"I'm sure Dayla won't leave the rock in her pod," I said, chewing noisily. I snatched up my floppy hat and shoved it on my head. "We'll have to go after her on that ArborQuest."

chapter eleven

As we left the building, Mr. Willoughby's head swung from side to side. His nostrils flared. His ears moved constantly. "How extraordinary! I seem to have sensors for everything. Things I've only accessed from my databanks are right here! Look, there's a saringa tree." He closed his eyes and inhaled deeply. "Can you smell those flowers? Marvelous."

I couldn't smell any flowers and I didn't know which of the scrubby trees was a saringa. Even so, I felt slightly superior. After all, I had several more hours' experience being Outside than Mr. Willoughby had.

"Let me know if you spot any coral spuds, Mr. Willoughby." I was panting slightly. The air was already getting hot again after last night's coolness. "Or any other creatures."

"I've spotted several interesting species already," Mr. Willoughby said.

I looked wildly around. "What creatures? Where?"

"Most are microscopic. My optical capabilities are excellent." He glanced at me. "None are a threat to human life. Why are you breathing so heavily?"

Mr. Willoughby wouldn't sound so calm if I was about to be attacked. "Well, it's hot and it's hard to walk in the sand."

"Why don't you ride?" He stopped sideways across my path. "I believe you grab my mane and pull yourself up."

"Is it okay? I mean, you're not really a robo horse."

"Yes, I am," Mr. Willoughby said cheerfully. "Hop up."

"I've never ridden a robo horse before." I'd taken Mom's robo horse apart, but I'd never tried to ride it. "You're very tall. I need something to stand on."

"Over there under the saringa tree." Mr. Willoughby headed for a fallen log under a tree with little heart-shaped leaves. Carefully I stepped up and balanced on the log. Then I pulled myself onto

Mr. Willoughby's back. I was up high, surrounded by drooping clusters of sweet-smelling purple flowers. The ground seemed far, far away.

"I don't like it up here." I leaned over and wrapped my arms around Mr. Willoughby's neck.

"Just relax and breathe," said Mr. Willoughby. "Isn't that scent exquisite?"

You can't help Mom and Star if you stay here, I scolded myself. I took a deep breath and inhaled the sweet, powdery smell of saringa flowers. *Nice,* I thought. Much better than air from an atmosphere controller.

I let go of Mr. Willoughby's neck and sat up cautiously. Being so high wasn't too bad once I got used to it. I could see every detail of the flowers when I was this close. Shades of purple, violet, and lilac combined in each flower. The violet was just the color of Star's hair; the leaves were the color of Zell's old-fashioned lace-ups. A scary thought popped into my head. Were the phony movers still trying to find me? I shivered before I remembered the barrier wall. There was no way they could get into Back to Basics School. If the wall didn't keep them out, the guards would. Star and I were safe.

"Okay, Mr. Willoughby. I'm ready."

Mr. Willoughby took a step forward, and I clutched his mane. He carried me out from under the saringa tree, across the dusty red sand, and through the red-brown trees wrapped with vines that he called hazelites. A bunch of kids on robo horses crowded around the human teacher in front of the class building.

A loud voice rose above the noise of the crowd.

"She won't show up. She's just a fluff-brain coward."

So Dayla thought she'd scared me away? I smiled. This would be fun.

I braced myself as Mr. Willoughby made his way into the crowd. But I could deal with real people when I was sitting up high like this.

We found Brash before we reached Dayla. He was standing at his horse's head, stroking its nose. The mud-brown horse had less intelligence in its eyes than Mr. Willoughby, but its coat was shining and its mane lay like a silk curtain on its neck.

"Hello, Brash," I said, riding up beside him. His hat was pulled down over his face, but he looked up at the sound of my voice. I leaned close. "Dayla has what I need. It's the pink rock."

Brash swung onto his horse, his survival belt clanking. He had a daypack on his back, and another lay across his horse's neck. "Do not be worrying. We'll get it back."

"So you decided to show up, Fluff Brain," Dayla said, riding over. Her daypack was stuffed so full it bulged like a hump on her back. She glanced at Mr. Willoughby and her eyes narrowed. "You'll be eating a lot of dust riding on that old thing."

I swallowed my temper. "Dayla, please give me my rock."

She raised her eyebrows, reached into her pocket, and drew out the pink rock. "Now, what's so important about you?" she asked it.

I grabbed but she shoved it back into her pocket. "It's mine now."

"Perhaps you would introduce me to this person, Tria?" Mr. Willoughby said, bobbing his head.

Dayla's eyes popped. "Y-your r-r-robo horse talks," she stammered.

"Of course." I winked at Brash. "Doesn't yours?"

Dayla stopped staring and tossed her head. "Oh, that dumb factory. My upgrade hasn't arrived yet. I'm sure it'll be here any day now."

"Excuse me." Mr. Willoughby held his head high. "You will not be receiving any upgrades that will make your robo horse like me. I am one of a kind. I am the only Mobile Away-from-Home Tutor."

Dayla's mouth opened and closed, but no sound came out.

"This fish mouth is Dayla, Mr. Willoughby." I turned. "And of course you remember Brash."

"Brash, how are you? Dayla, nice to meet you."

"Well, maybe he can talk," Dayla said, recovering. "But he's just an old piece of junk. You'll be eating my dust."

"Will not!"

"Will so!"

"Class, it's time to start," Ms. Linden called. "Tria, wait just a moment. You need a daypack."

Dayla spun her horse, pushed through the crowd, and galloped off to the west.

"Let's go," I whispered to Mr. Willoughby and Brash.

Mr. Willoughby stood firm. "Your teacher has said you may not leave yet, Tria."

"I have a pack for her." Brash pointed to the day-pack across his horse's neck.

Ms. Linden threaded her way over to us. "Excellent. Good luck today."

"Allow me to introduce myself," said Mr. Willoughby, courteously dipping his head at Ms. Linden. "I am the first Mobile Away-from-Home Tutor. Soon you will be able to read about my experiences in the body of a robo horse."

"But this is dreadful!" Ms. Linden gazed into

Mr. Willoughby's eyes. "No teacher, even an Artificial Intelligence, should be made to live as an animal. I'll take you to our lab. I'm sure our science teacher can restore you to your former self."

"Don't you touch him!" I said, flinging my arms around Mr. Willoughby's neck.

"I like being the first Mobile Away-from-Home Tutor." Mr. Willoughby continued earnestly. "More can be accomplished when one is interacting with pupils outside of a scholarly environment."

Ms. Linden hesitated. "Well, perhaps . . . I must consult with the other teachers."

"Please." Brash nudged his horse forward. "We are needing to leave on the ArborQuest."

"We have to catch up to our teammate," I said, hoping to remind Ms. Linden of her goal of team-work.

Ms. Linden looked uncertainly at Mr. Willoughby. But then she gave in. "Very well. We'll speak again when you return."

I pulled the daypack onto my shoulders.

"It should be simple to catch Dayla." Brash pointed. "She'll have to return. She's going in the wrong direction."

Brash and I walked our robo horses after Dayla.

"She'll come galloping back any minute," I said firmly. "And then I'll make her give me that rock."

But Dayla didn't return, and I started to get nervous. "Maybe she's working with the kidnappers," I burst out. "She's taking the device to them."

"Don't let your imagination run away with you, Tria," Mr. Willoughby said, plodding steadily along. "She's just an ordinary girl. Although"—his ears flicked nervously—"she is taking a long time."

"Perhaps we should hurry," Brash suggested.

I clutched Mr. Willoughby's mane and tightened my grip on his sides. "Can you go faster, Mr. Willoughby?"

Mr. Willoughby flowed into an easy swinging gait. I loosened my grip a little and let myself relax and rock with the motion.

"Cantering is my favorite," Brash called, grinning at me. His robo horse was moving side by side with Mr. Willoughby. Brash wasn't even holding on to the mane.

Mr. Willoughby flung up his head and pricked his ears forward. "What's this? Telescopic vision? Yes, very useful. Dayla is waiting for us by the wall."

A few minutes later we saw Dayla casually leaning against the brown barrier wall. Her robo horse stood immobile beside her. With an air of mild interest, she watched us canter up and stop in front of her.

"What took you so long?" She yawned delicately and patted her mouth.

I swung off Mr. Willoughby. "Give me the rock," I growled, advancing on her. "Give it to me or Mr. Willoughby will sit on you."

Dayla straightened abruptly and put out both hands to fend me off. "I don't know why you're so upset. You can have the stupid rock."

I looked at her suspiciously. It couldn't be this easy. "Hand it over, then."

She grinned, and I knew I'd been right not to trust her. "You'll have to go get it. I threw it over the wall."

chapter twelve

"You what?" I howled, and rushed at her. She dodged behind Brash's horse.

"You can get it," she said breathlessly. "Just open the gate."

I spun and looked more closely at the wall. Sure enough, there was a keypad with the telltale red lights flickering. I unbuttoned my pocket and pulled out my WonderTool.

"Wait." Brash slid off his horse and marched up to Dayla. He tipped back his hat and squinted at her. "How could you throw something over the wall? It is too high."

"You are correct, Brash," Mr. Willoughby said judiciously. He eyed the wall. "It measures almost twenty meters."

"Okay, okay." Dayla shrugged. "I used a popper."

She pulled a cheap toy propulsion gun from her pocket and waved it around. "Only one pop left."

Brash frowned. "Another forbidden technology."

Furious, I powered up the WonderTool and stepped over to her robo horse. I reached between its ears, flicked the Off switch, opened a seam, and loosened a connection.

"Hey, what are you doing?" Dayla yelled.

"I'm turning off your horse." I shook the Wonder-Tool at her. "You're not going anywhere until I have that rock." My voice rose. "How do I know you're even telling the truth? You're always making trouble."

To my astonishment, Dayla turned red and looked down. "Why does everyone always say that?" She raised her head. "I'm sure Dad didn't mean it, though. Besides, I don't see what's so wrong with telling the Cruxor ambassador that his cook was serving spoiled food. That was the stinkiest stuff I ever smelled. How was I to know it was *supposed* to smell like that?"

"You're worried about spoiled food. I'm worried about saving my mother." I turned my back on her and bent close to study the wall's keypad.

"I don't know what you're talking about," Dayla complained.

Mr. Willoughby and Brash began explaining, but I

concentrated on getting the gate open. Once I had the rock, Mr. Willoughby and I could leave.

"Why did you throw the rock?" Brash asked.

"So I can get out, of course." The superior tone had returned to Dayla's voice. "As soon as I saw that robo horse, I knew Fluff Brain had a tool that would get me through that gate."

I started removing the front of the keypad.

"Running away is never a good idea," Mr. Willoughby said sympathetically.

"I'm not running away!" Dayla sounded exasperated. "There's a bilo tree not far from here. I'm going to get that leaf and win. Once I'm a winner, Dad will forgive me and let me come home again."

I eased the WonderTool around a red wire and tried to focus. The lock on the Administrator's office hadn't been this difficult. I removed a chip, and suddenly the lights flashed green and the barrier wall opened.

"Good for you, Fluff Brain," Dayla said. "Your criminal ability is almost as good as my brains."

I shook my head. "You've got that backward." I shut off the WonderTool and buttoned it safely into my pocket. "Come on, let's find my rock."

Brash led his horse through the gate. Dayla's

horse remained behind, of course, since I'd turned it off. Mr. Willoughby stood outside the gate with us, swiveling his head from side to side.

In front of us was a sea of red sand and hazelite vines. And nuts. Thousands of hard brown nuts lay scattered all over the sand. Bushes full of them grew in clumps outside the wall.

"Look at this!" I was horrified. "We'll never find the rock!"

"Well, I didn't know about the nuts, did I?" Dayla said defensively. She kicked hard at a pile of nuts and they went flying.

"We'll find it," Mr. Willoughby said in his deep, soothing voice. "Just search slowly and methodically."

Dayla was under a bush, Mr. Willoughby was searching along the wall, and I was crawling through the sand when Brash called triumphantly, "I've found a pink rock!"

We rushed over, and I snatched it up. "Yes, this is it." I squeezed the pink rock tight and felt a tide of relief flow through me. "Now we can go rescue Mom!"

"Tria, may I see it more closely?" Mr. Willoughby bumped my hand with his nose, and I obediently opened my fist. He turned his head sideways and scrutinized the rock with one eye. He dropped his head closer, rolled the stone over with his nose, and then moved his head slowly back and forth, examining it first with one eye, then the other.

"What is your horse doing, Fluff Brain?" Dayla scoffed.

Suddenly Mr. Willoughby threw up his head, eyes wide, ears alert. "Quick, someone's coming. Back through the gate!"

Brash immediately leaped onto his horse, but when Mr. Willoughby shoved me toward the gate, I tripped and fell.

"I don't hear anything," Dayla said loftily, not moving.

A big black air car glided up and sank to the ground.

"Run!" I screamed, trying to scramble to my feet.

But we were too slow. The air car's door popped open, and two feet in old-fashioned green lace-ups appeared, followed by an arm holding a stunner.

"How nice of you to come meet us," Zell said, aiming her weapon directly at me. "Chip, guard the gate so they don't get any foolish ideas."

Chip pushed his black hair out of his eyes, pulled out his stunner, and moved to the gate.

I glared at Dayla. "You led us here," I accused. "You betrayed us!"

Dayla looked shocked. "I did not!" she yelled. "I just want to win ArborQuest. I don't know these people!"

I knew they were after Star. They wanted her to tell them where the device was. I backed slowly toward Mr. Willoughby, hiding the pink stone behind me.

"Hand it over," Zell said. "I know you have the disk."

Beside me, Mr. Willoughby dropped his head and nosed around in the nuts. Zell swung her weapon toward him. "What's he doing?"

"He's looking for food to eat," Brash said softly.

"Robo horses don't eat!" called Chip.

Mr. Willoughby's sides were puffing in and out, in and out. I looked at him in alarm. "I think he's sick."

We all stared at him. Mr. Willoughby whipped up his head, pursed his lips, and *whoosh!* he blew a nut right at Zell, whacking her on the forehead. *Whoosh!* A second nut hit her hand, and her weapon fell to the ground.

"I must have included the bellows and blower from the residence cleaner in him," I murmured in astonishment.

Mr. Willoughby wheeled and shot two more nuts at Chip. *Whoosh, whoosh!* Then, without stopping to see Chip's reaction, he shouted, "Get up quick! Go, Brash!"

Brash took off at a gallop away from the school while Dayla and I scrambled onto Mr. Willoughby's broad back. Dayla made it up first and yanked me up behind her. I wrapped my arms tightly around her waist as we bounded forward.

Mr. Willoughby galloped to the air car and launched two well-aimed kicks at it. The car's hood crunched and buckled. Then we, too, were racing away down a beaten sand path.

Sand exploded beside us. A noise crashed in my ears, louder even than when I'd zapped out our building's power grid. They didn't have stunners. That had to be the noise of a blaster. Mr. Willoughby put on an additional burst of speed and we were safely away, my ears still ringing.

We caught up with Brash, and the two robo horses rushed on and on. Finally Mr. Willoughby slowed as the path narrowed.

"We've lost them for now," he said, stopping and surveying the path behind us. "And I believe I disabled their car quite effectively."

"I knew it," Brash said, a huge grin splitting his face. "You are a most marvelous horse."

I dismounted and went to stand on shaky legs at Mr. Willoughby's head. "Thank you, Mr. Willoughby." I hugged his neck. "You saved us."

He nodded. "I believe I did." He pointed his nose at the sky and his eyes took on a dreamy look. "My first article will be entitled 'How to Save Your Students While in Pursuit of Educational Goals.' "

"Sure. Whatever you say." I pulled the rock from my pocket. "Now we can head for town and save Mom."

Mr. Willoughby lost his dreamy look. "Tria, I don't think—"

"Oh no you don't!" Dayla dug her heels into Mr. Willoughby's sides. "Come on, horse. The bilo tree's supposed to be right over that hill. We're going to win."

Mr. Willoughby didn't move, of course.

"Stop kicking him!" I shouted. "He's a person. And forget about your stupid bilo tree. We have to save my mother."

While I was speaking, Brash sidestepped his

horse over. "Do not kick Mr. Willoughby." He tipped back his hat and glared at Dayla.

Dayla grimaced. "All right already. I won't kick him. But it'll just take a second to go get the leaf."

"No," Brash and I said together. We exchanged satisfied looks.

Mr. Willoughby rested his head on my shoulder and nuzzled my hair. "I have some bad news. We don't have the device. The rock is just . . . a rock."

chapter thirteen

I **opened** my fist and stared at the rock in disbelief. "But Star said . . ." My voice trailed away. Actually I didn't know what Star said. It had sounded like "pink rock." Or was it "pink red" after all? A flood of misery rushed over me.

"I examined it with my microscopic vision," Mr. Willoughby explained. "It's a Chiron rock. Nothing unusual."

I closed my fingers around the rock's jagged edges and squeezed until it hurt. "We'll go to town anyway. We need to find a holo projector and hear what Star is really saying."

"Yes." Mr. Willoughby took his head off my shoulder and gave me a little nudge. "Get back on. Dayla will help you."

Instead, Dayla slid off. "I don't want to go to

town. I want to win ArborQuest. That bilo tree is right over this hill, and I'm going to find it."

I hauled myself onto Mr. Willoughby. "You and your stupid ArborQuest. Go ahead, then. We won't miss you."

"We must stay together," Mr. Willoughby said. "The maps say the earthcrust is very unstable. Only the paths are safe."

Uneasily I examined the sandy red path under us. It looked solid enough. But so did the shiny black rock I could see off to the side.

"I'm not a great hulking robo horse," Dayla said, stepping off the path. "It's not as if the earth is going to open up and swallow me."

"Come back, Dayla," Mr. Willoughby said.

"No." She turned and marched away from the path. "I'm going to win."

Brash slid off his horse. "Tria, you have Mr. Willoughby. Dayla is alone. I will go with her. Good luck in town."

"Brash, no."

But Brash waved and quickly caught up with Dayla as she climbed the hill.

I watched them go with mixed feelings. I didn't want them to get hurt, but I didn't want to hang around and waste time either. Mr. Willoughby balanced on the edge of the path. "Come back!" he called. "It's not safe!"

They crested the hill and disappeared. Then we heard Dayla's triumphant voice.

"There's the tree! I was right!"

I grabbed Mr. Willoughby's mane as he took off up the path. It curved away from Dayla and Brash but it led to the top of the hill. I didn't try to stop him. I wanted to see what was on the other side, too.

Clumps of scrubby brush and a few plumes of tall grass lay before us. Brash and Dayla were running toward a huge tree.

"See?" she yelled. "Perfectly safe."

Then—*crack!* the earth opened, and Dayla and Brash disappeared in a cloud of dust.

"Brash! Dayla!" I called frantically. "They're dead! I should have known this was going to happen. We never should have come Outside!"

"Tria! Be sensible." Mr. Willoughby nudged my leg with his nose. "Not everyone who goes Outside dies. We don't know what's happened."

"So we can save them?" Hope leaped up in me. "Hurry, Mr. Willoughby!"

He didn't move. "No, Tria. I suspect that only a thin earthcrust covers hollow chambers beneath. We too could go crashing through the ground at any moment. We cannot leave the path. The best thing is to go back for help." He started to turn.

"No! We can't leave them." I leaned forward on his neck, as if I could cross that treacherous ground by sheer willpower. "If only you could fly!"

"Fly?" Mr. Willoughby tilted his head and considered. "I'm still getting used to this body, but let me see . . ."

Suddenly Mr. Willoughby and I were rocking and teetering above the ground.

"Aah!" I screamed, clutching his mane.

"I can't stabilize!" But even as he said it, Mr. Willoughby stopped rocking and rolling, and I was sitting on a quiet horse again.

I looked down. We were only a few centimeters off the ground. I let go of Mr. Willoughby's mane and patted his neck.

"I guess I mixed the Fly-by-night into you, too. You are some fabulous robo horse! Let's go!"

Slowly we floated out over the unstable ground. We were so low that plumes of feathery grass brushed at Mr. Willoughby's legs.

"Can't you go any faster? And higher? I remember the Fly-by-night swooped around way up high."

"The Fly-by-night," said Mr. Willoughby calmly, "was much smaller and only carried its sonar. We are too heavy to go higher or faster."

I twined my fingers in Mr. Willoughby's mane and leaned forward, craning to see if there were any signs of Brash and Dayla. There was nothing. I was surprised to feel a tear trickling down my cheek. Who would think I'd be so upset about two real people? Especially when one of them was Dayla.

The dust was still settling when we finally floated up to the hole. Such a small hole for so much dust!

I gulped. A floppy white hat lay near the opening, half covered by dirt and rocks. I tore my eyes away from the hat and saw a vine hanging over the edge of the hole. The other end was tangled in the branches of the bilo tree.

"Look, Mr. Willoughby!" I leaned over his neck and pointed. "That vine must lead down to Brash and Dayla!"

"Now, don't get too excited," Mr. Willoughby cautioned. "We need to think this through."

"It's just like the Sewers of Plato vid! You slide down the vine and land safely in the underground city." I was already sliding off his back. But as soon as my feet touched the earth, it crumpled—and I crashed through.

I landed with a thud, and chunks of earth fell in on top of me. I lay still for a moment, trying to catch my breath. AlmostReality was much better than reality. Reality hurt! With a grunt, I pushed a rock off my chest and spat out some dirt.

"Tria!"

I tried to answer Mr. Willoughby but started sneezing instead. "Ah-choo! *Ah-choo!*"

"You could power an engine with that sneeze, Fluff Brain. Did you get a bilo leaf?"

"Dayla!"

The lump of sand that was Dayla groaned and sat up. I rolled to my knees and crawled over to her. "Are you all right?"

"Yes." Dayla shook the dust out of her hair and blinked at me.

"Tria!" Mr. Willoughby stuck his head through the broken earthcrust, blocking the light.

"I'm okay," I called, gazing up at him.

"What about Brash and Dayla?"

"Dayla's okay. Brash—"

"Here I am." A shadowy figure stumbled over, survival belt clanking, and dropped down beside us.

"The hole is too small for me to come through," Mr. Willoughby called. "I'll have to go for help. Take care of each other. I won't be long."

Light flooded down again as he moved away.

"Hurry!" I yelled. "I need to be in town by noon." We were running out of time. But I could count on Mr. Willoughby. He'd get us out of here.

"Was he *flying?*" Dayla stared up at the hole.

"Most marvelous," Brash breathed.

"Humph!" Dayla said. "Why didn't you get us a leaf?"

Unbelievable. I shook my head and turned to Brash. His clothes were filthy and torn, and he had skinned knuckles and a cut on his forehead. Since Dayla was equally scraped and dirty, I figured I looked pretty much like them. At least Star was still safe in my shoe.

"We were fine until you fell on top of us." Dayla slid her daypack off her shoulders.

"Oh. Sorry. I was *rescuing* you."

Brash coughed. "Thank you."

We were in a large chamber, with rocks and dirt and sand all around. At least this ground felt solid. I hoped I was safe from germs and creatures down here.

I heard the jangling of Brash's survival belt, and then a bright light spread around us.

"Logen candle," Brash said, lowering the brightness a bit.

I smiled in relief. Now no creatures could sneak up on me. "That Administrator was wrong! We do need your belt here."

"What we need," Dayla said, rummaging through her pack, "is a bilo leaf." With a disgusted sigh, she upended her pack and dumped everything out. She pulled a notebook from the pile. "Okay, did either of you observe any hyperweed infestation?"

I looked at her in disbelief.

She raised her eyebrows. "I didn't see any, did you?"

I shook my head.

"No," said Brash.

"No weeds." She wrote carefully with her pen.

"Don't you have a word screen for writing?" I asked, peering over to see what real pen writing looked like.

"Don't be silly. This is Back to Basics School." She leaned her notebook on her knee and chewed on the end of the pen. "Now I just have to record the coordinates and all that stuff."

Dayla started scribbling in her notebook, and I turned to Brash with a sigh. "Are you okay? You could clean up that cut if you have one of those water bubbles left."

"Water is for drinking during emergencies." Brash

twisted his survival belt around, reached into one of the pouches, and pulled out a small cloth. He pressed it to his cut, wincing.

"Healing cloth," he said, noticing my questioning look. "Kills germs."

"Germs!" I watched him anxiously, hoping he'd killed the germs quickly enough.

He gestured to my pack. "Look in there."

I'd forgotten all about the lightweight daypack on my back. I pulled it off and dumped it out. Unlike Dayla's overstuffed one, mine only had a few things in it. "Sandwiches! Water!" Greedily I uncapped the water and took a few gulps. Then I unwrapped the sandwiches and started eating.

Brash was eating, too, and taking quick sips from his water bottle. He looked perfectly calm and self-possessed, and his cut had stopped bleeding.

I looked at him curiously. "Guess you're used to being Outside?"

He nodded happily. "I am Outside a lot with my furbeasts." His expression darkened. "Until my parents decided I needed more education and I received a grant to come here. So many people, so much noise. And we are always inside. So boring—nothing to do." He grinned at me. "It is much better since you are here. It is not boring at all."

"No," I agreed. "It's not boring." That reminded me of my problems. "Brash, I have to get to town."

Brash was staring past me at Dayla. I looked over. She was still scribbling away.

"You are in need of a holo projector," he said slowly, "to listen to Star?"

"Right." I wondered what he was thinking.

"Dayla has a projector," he said softly.

Maybe that cut on his head was worse than I'd realized. "You told me it was confiscated."

"The blue one was taken away. But not that one." He picked up the light and pointed it directly at Dayla.

And there, in the pile of things from her daypack, was a shiny new holo projector.

chapter fourteen

I **pounced.** I grabbed the projector and yanked it toward me like a lifeline. Which it was.

"Hey!" shouted Dayla. "That's mine!" She dropped her notebook and pen and lunged for the projector.

"Please!" I gasped, hugging it tight. "I have to hear Star's message. It's a matter of life and death."

"Yeah, right." She pulled at the projector.

"We have already told you that," Brash said sharply, moving to stand beside me.

"Well, I haven't already believed you," Dayla mocked him. She continued tugging and pulling, but I curled my body around the projector and hung on.

Dayla must have accidentally hit a switch, because suddenly a small blue rabbit appeared and wiggled its ears at Dayla. "How ya doing?"

I stared in disbelief at the Bunny Friend. "The old blue projector was yours!"

"Hi!" said the rabbit. "I'm Benjamin. Who are you?"

Dayla stopped fighting me for the projector. "Benjamin, this is Tria." Dayla stuck out her chin, like she was daring me to laugh. "And you already met Brash."

"Hello, Benjamin," Brash said awkwardly.

Dayla's voice turned gruff. "Just wanted to let you know I'm okay. See you again in a little bit."

Dayla reached between my arms and turned off the projector. "Don't you say a word," she growled. "My mother gave Benjamin to me. Since she left, he's the only one who'll talk to me about her. My father refuses to even speak her name." She slitted her eyes and curled her hands into fists. "If you tell the Administrator, I'll—"

"I won't." I put the projector down on a rock. I sympathized with Dayla, but I was still determined to see Star. "Do you want to take Benjamin out, or shall I?"

I expected her to keep fighting me, but Dayla sighed and carefully removed Benjamin's disk. She carried it to her daypack pile, wrapped it in a blue silk cloth, placed the cloth in a matching blue drawstring bag, and gently drew the strings closed.

I couldn't believe I'd been this close to a projector all along. I pulled off my shoe and fished Star out.

"You keep her in your shoe? What kind of friend are you, Fluff Brain?" Dayla sounded genuinely shocked. I didn't answer. My heart was beating fast with anticipation.

This projector was new and of the highest quality. Star's disk dropped softly into the slot, and I quickly turned it on.

Star appeared, violet eyes finding me right away. We smiled at each other, and I felt all bright inside, like I'd swallowed Brash's candle.

"Nice outfit," Dayla said.

"Hi, Star!" I said, ignoring her.

"Hi! Did you find the device?" She glanced at Dayla and Brash, her eyes moving over the ceiling and floor of our cavern. "Tria?" Her voice was apprehensive. "This doesn't look good. Are these people . . . friendly?"

I rushed to reassure her. "Oh, yes!" Then I glanced at Dayla. "Well, some of the time."

Dayla squinched up her face at me.

"Star, that's Dayla and this is Brash. They're real.

But I don't have the device. I couldn't hear your message."

Star's shoulders slumped. "That's bad. We'll have to work quickly. Tria, you remember the Olympian vase?"

I nodded.

"Hidden in the vase is a grayish pink wedge about this big." Star held up her thumb to show how big it was.

Pink wedge. Not "pink red" or "pink rock."

"So what's so great about a pink wedge?" Dayla smirked.

Star's eyes locked on mine. "It's a device that will make holograms solid."

No one spoke. We all stared at Star. Something thumped overhead, and a shower of pebbles and dirt came down the hole. None of us even looked up.

Finally Dayla said, "If that's true, Benjamin could be real!"

Star frowned. "If Benjamin is a hologram, I can assure you he's already real!"

"Star," I whispered. My brain was spinning and I felt like I'd just been given the best present in the whole world. "It's what I've been waiting for. You . . . you could be solid. You wouldn't *need* a projector."

Star shook her head, and all the joy drained out of me. "I told you before, Tria. I'm happy the way I am. Besides, you're not thinking this through. If holograms can be made solid, think of hologram bombs and hologram armies that could suddenly become solid. The destruction would be terrible."

Brash stared at Star in horror. "My brother is a Planetary Guard. I do not want suddenly solid hologram bombs going off near him! We must keep that device out of the wrong hands."

Star nodded. "Exactly. This could be a weapon of mass destruction. You could take over worlds with this. Billions of lives are at stake."

"We could rule the galaxy," Dayla said, her face glowing with enthusiasm. "We could make sure holograms everywhere were treated with respect. We could—"

"Dayla!" Brash's voice was sharp. "This is not a game."

Dayla stomped her foot. "I know it's not! This is important."

I agreed with her totally. Well, maybe not the "rule the galaxy" part, but the rest of it. I was starting to say so when Star spoke softly.

"Dayla, I appreciate what you're saying, but we can't keep the device."

Somehow I'd known she'd say that.

Dayla's face darkened, but then she turned to me. "We could at least make Benjamin and Star solid so they could be at school with us."

My heart said *yes!* But my head knew better. "Star doesn't want to be solid. And this device is too dangerous for us to keep. We need to find it and save Mom."

Star sighed. "I'm glad you understand, Tria. Is the Olympian vase close by?"

"It's in my pod at school," I said slowly, still thinking wistfully of a solid Star. It was hard to let that dream go. "It's safe, but we have to hurry. I have to get to town by noon to save Mom."

"Thank you for telling me where the device is," a voice called mockingly. The ground above us rumbled and shook.

My blood ran cold. On the edge of the hole stood a pair of feet in old-fashioned green lace-ups.

Zell.

She laughed and moved away, the ground thudding with each step. We covered our heads as dirt and rocks loosened and fell.

"Chip," we heard her say. "Don't let them out of that hole."

"We have to stop her!" Star's voice popped and

crackled. I spun to look at her. She was flickering in and out. And then she was gone.

"Star!" I ran for the projector. I couldn't stand losing her again. "This is a new projector. What's wrong with it? Whatever it is, I'll fix it."

"We have no time." Brash's voice jolted me back to reality. "We must rescue your mother and stop the thief!"

Dayla grabbed the projector. "It's a solar cell and needs to be recharged, Fluff Brain."

"There's still a piece of vine hanging down," I said, focusing on the first and most important thing to do. "Boost me up so I can grab it."

Dayla sat down on a rock. "Sure. And then Chippie pushes you back in, and this time you break a leg or, even worse, you land on me and *I* break a leg."

I plopped down beside Dayla. How were we going to get out of here?

"Chip!" Brash threw a rock out the hole. "Are you there?"

"Yeah?" The voice came from directly overhead.

Brash peered up at the opening. "You must help us."

"Zell said no." The voice retreated.

I sat up straight as an idea occurred to me.

"That's funny," Dayla said, staring upward.

I looked at her. Was she thinking the same thing?

"He's walking around," I said. "But . . ."

"But the ground isn't shaking," Dayla said, picking up on my thought. "The earth isn't crumbling, pebbles aren't falling."

We nodded at each other. "He's a hologram."

"Oh no." Brash groaned. "I am remembering the last time Tria thought a guard was a hologram."

Dayla snorted with laughter. "We heard about that at breakfast. Pretty funny."

I stood and brushed the dirt off my uniform. "Brash, boost me up."

Brash didn't move. "You are going to get hurt."

Dayla heaved a heavy sigh. "Am I the only one with brains? Let's make a pile of rocks and you can stand on that."

We piled the biggest rocks we could find on the sturdy floor of the chamber. We stood on the pile, and Brash and Dayla steadied me as I jumped for the end of the vine. It took three tries before I got it.

"Give me a boost so I can start climbing."

Dust and pebbles showered down on me as I pulled on the vine. Below me Dayla and Brash pushed. Hand over hand I hauled myself up. I wished I had my gloves. The vine bit into the palms of my hands, and my shoulder muscles stabbed with pain.

"Hey, what's going on down there?" Chip's voice was right above me. I kept climbing, though my hands were starting to cramp.

"You try to come out of that hole and I'll push you back in."

"I hope I'm right about you," I muttered. I was at the top! I grabbed the side of the hole with one hand, and it crumbled. I snatched at the vine again and held on while dirt tumbled past me.

"Be careful! You're going to bury us down here!"

Carefully, slowly, I inched up . . . and over.

chapter fifteen

"If I shoot you, you'll never be able to rescue your mother," Chip threatened.

A blaster was pointed right at me. "If I stay here I can't rescue her, either," I said defiantly.

"You don't need to." Chip waved the weapon airily. "The Captain hired us to bring him the device. You're just a backup plan. Once we sell the device to the Captain, he won't need your mother anymore. Maybe he'll let her go." Chip shook his head. "And maybe not. My advice is don't go anywhere near him. The man's dangerous. And his doctor friend is insane." Chip stood up. "I'm doing you a favor keeping you here, where you're safe."

Insane? Dangerous? What was happening to Mom? I had to get out of this hole. "You're a hologram! And your weapon can't hurt me." Maybe if I said it loudly enough I'd make it true.

Chip narrowed his eyes and pointed the blaster at my forehead. "Are you willing to take that chance?"

I closed my eyes, thought of Mom, thought about the school guards, thought about the way Chip was walking safely around on a thin earthcrust, and whispered, "Yes."

I started to wriggle farther out, and there was an explosion of sound and light. I flinched but felt no pain. There wasn't even any sand flying up in my face. Relief made me weak. He was a hologram.

"What's going on? Tria, are you all right?" Brash and Dayla called anxiously.

"I'm okay!" I yelled. "He's a hologram."

"No, I'm not!"

I squirmed and pulled myself up until my whole body was flat on the ground. I lay there, breathing hard. I dragged myself a few feet more and finally dared to sit up.

Chip's holographic projector was tucked securely under the overhang of a rock. If I could get to it, I could have Star back right away. I started to crawl forward, but the ground rumbled and I froze.

Chip stood watching me, weapon hanging limp at

his side. "I let her down," he said flatly. "I let Zell down."

"Well, you shouldn't be trying to trap people in holes and steal things from them anyway," I said unsympathetically. "You're as bad as the Captain."

Chip holstered his weapon. "We are not. We're not planning to raise armies and take over the worlds like he is. Zell just wants to make me solid and sell the device to the Captain for a lot of money."

"I'd like to make my friend Star solid, but you don't see me shooting and stealing, do you?"

Chip shrugged.

The vine gave a jerk and tightened. "Push, Brash, push!" Suddenly Dayla's head popped out of the hole. She gave a squeak of alarm as the edge crumbled some more.

"Lie flat!" I called. "Go slow."

In a minute Dayla was lying near me, puffing and breathless, and Brash started squirming out after her. Still lying flat, Dayla pulled her projector from her pack. "Gotta get it recharged. Now, where's that bilo tree?"

Then she spotted Chip's projector. "Look! I can have Benjamin back right away!" She tried to jump up, but her foot popped through the earthcrust and the ground cracked and broke around it.

"Get down!" I yelled, hugging the ground. Quickly Dayla spread herself flat again. Brash froze, his feet still hanging over the edge of the hole. The three of us didn't dare move.

Chip walked around, looking at us. He smiled. "Good. You have to stay here, just like Zell wanted."

A shadow fell on us as we lay immobile on the ground. It wasn't Chip. Holograms don't have shadows. Whatever it was made a raspy buzz as it came.

"Here comes Zell," Chip said.

The big black air car choked and coughed up to the rock overhang. Mr. Willoughby's hooves had left two big dents on the car's hood, and from the sound of it, in the car's engine, too. The door creaked open, and Zell leaned out. "Kid, you've got the messiest pod I've ever seen. But it's a lot cleaner now." She held up a bulging pillowcase, and I closed my eyes in despair. "I took everything that might be the device," she told Chip.

Chip hurried into the car as Zell grabbed his projector. "Soon you'll be solid," she said to him. "We'll test all of these before we sell the right one to the Captain."

"Wait!" I said, though I knew it was hopeless. "You have to help me save my mother."

Zell glanced at me impatiently, and then her gaze

sharpened. "Well, well, what do we have here?" She backed the air car jerkily over to us and, before we realized her intentions, scooped up Dayla's projector—with Star's disk still inside.

"Star!" I tried to lunge, but my knee popped through the earthcrust and I fell flat on my face.

"You can't have too many projectors around," Zell said cheerfully. "Especially new up-to-the-minute ones like this." Zell slammed the door, and the big car careened unsteadily away, spraying sand over us.

I scarcely noticed the sand stinging my hands. It couldn't be true. It wasn't true.

She'd stolen Star.

Star, with her silly outfits and her love of birds. Star, who encouraged me when I tried to climb new terrains and worried when I fell. Star, who always helped me when I was in trouble. Star, my best friend. I imagined Zell opening the projector, seeing Star's disk, and tossing it out into the red sand. Star would be lost forever.

I cried. Great sobs shook my whole body and made the earth rumble beneath me. I didn't care, I just wept harder. I wailed and pounded the ground and tried to smash a hole in the earthcrust. But nothing took the pain away and gradually I ran out of energy. All that was left were the tears that poured quietly down my face.

I rolled over and sat up. The ground trembled and cracked, but no holes opened up. I didn't disappear. Too bad.

"Watch it, Fluff Brain." Dayla's voice sounded softer than usual. "You're going to bury us all again."

Brash's feet were still in the hole, and he was lying on his belly. "Do not worry. We will get Star back."

Dayla brushed her hair out of her face and nodded. "We'll tell the Administrator what happened, Fluff Brain. And Mr. Willoughby!"

"Mr. Willoughby's probably being dismantled by those teachers," I choked out.

"No, I'm not."

My heart leaped. I twisted around to see a robo horse floating behind me. "Mr. Willoughby!" I jumped up and wrapped my arms around his neck. The ground started rumbling and cracking, so I pulled myself onto his back.

"Zell took Star." I swallowed hard and blinked back more tears.

Mr. Willoughby turned his neck to look at me. His

eyes glinted with determination. "We'll get Star back, I promise."

Dayla stared as we floated over to her. Then she cleared her throat. "About time you got here. Fluff Brain was trying to start another cave-in."

In spite of that remark, I held out my hand and helped her up.

"Most marvelous," Brash said, scrambling up behind Dayla when we reached him.

"I hid in the bushes when the car passed me the first time, but when it passed me again, heading in your direction, I came back. Now I'm returning you all to the safety of the school," Mr. Willoughby said firmly.

"No! We have to go to town," I protested. "Besides, school's not safe for *you*—those teachers want to dismantle you."

"It will take several hours to follow these paths to town. And we don't have several hours." Mr. Willoughby stuck his nose in the air. "I believe I can deal with the teachers."

"Wait!" Dayla screeched. "Get the leaf first!" She pointed at the bilo tree, and Mr. Willoughby obediently floated close to a branch. Dayla snatched off a few leaves.

As we floated slowly back to the path, I explained what had happened.

"Zell stole everything in my pod that might be the device. Star says the real device is a pink wedge. But I guess Zell didn't hear Star describe it, or she wouldn't have taken so many other things."

Mr. Willoughby landed on the path, ready to run. I talked quickly. "So you have to take me to town right away. Dayla and Brash can go back to school on Brash's horse."

Brash put two fingers in his mouth and gave a shrill whistle. We heard the pounding of hooves as Brash's robo horse raced up to us.

He grinned at the stunned look on our faces. "It is good to train your animals to come when you call." He slid off Mr. Willoughby's back and hopped onto his horse. "Come on, Dayla."

"Honestly, Fluff Brain," Dayla complained as she dropped to the ground. "Wouldn't it be faster to go to town in our air car?"

I felt like a red hot wire had just zapped me. "You have an air car, too?"

"It's not mine exactly. But it will be." Dayla climbed onto Brash's horse and put on her most superior expression. "The Administrator is taking the winning ArborQuest team to town in the school's convertible. He loves that old car like a baby. And it's faster than a robo horse."

Brash nodded eagerly. "Much faster."

Why hadn't I known about this? But this was no time to complain. "You win, Mr. Willoughby. Take us back to school."

We galloped the whole way back, stopping only long enough at the gate for me to reactivate Dayla's horse and let her climb aboard.

A crowd of teachers was waiting by the class building. Some were sitting under the saringa tree, fanning themselves with the heart-shaped leaves. I surveyed them nervously, looking for WonderTools or other signs of hostility.

"Welcome back!" Ms. Linden smiled her big-toothed smile. "May I have your report?"

"Tria's mother has been kidnapped and you have to send help for her." Dayla swung off her robo horse and rushed up to Ms. Linden. Digging into her pack, Dayla pulled out the leaf and the report. "We need our trip to town right away."

Ms. Linden took the leaf and report from Dayla. "I'm sorry, but you're the second team back. Meta's team won." Our teacher pushed her straw hat more firmly onto her head and looked at me. "Tria, we need to talk to Mr. Willoughby now."

"We lost?" Dayla yelled. "But I have to win!"

Ms. Linden shook her head reprovingly. "There are more important things than winning."

"You are right," Brash said softly. "You must help Tria's kidnapped mother."

A stout red-faced teacher pulled a WonderTool out of her pocket and stepped forward. "The Administrator warned us that Tria made up stories. Before she goes any further, we must restore her Home Tutor."

chapter sixteen

Dayla dashed over to stand in front of Mr. Willoughby. Brash jumped off his horse and stood beside her. I looked down at the press of bodies and hesitated. Then I slid off Mr. Willoughby and stood with Brash and Dayla. We were a solid wall between Mr. Willoughby and the stout teacher.

"Stand aside, children."

We didn't move. A sweat drop rolled down the teacher's red face and she wiped it away with an impatient hand. And then she reached to push me aside.

Pudgy germ-laden fingers came at me, and I almost dodged out of the way. But she was not going to get Mr. Willoughby. *Biopreventives*, I reminded myself, and squeezed my eyes shut.

Something hot and heavy landed with a meaty

thwack on my arm. An image of a giant corrosive mega-germ flashed into my head. *It's just a hand. A moist hand. A sweaty, germ-dripping . . . can't move, have to hold on for Mr. Willoughby . . . a perspiring, disease-spreading . . .*

The teacher spun away, and I almost collapsed in relief. But she darted to the side, and Brash and Dayla moved to block her. I tried to move, but I was too slow. She slipped in behind us and laid a hand on Mr. Willoughby's neck.

"Come with me," she soothed. "I'm a whiz with a WonderTool—I'll have you back to your old self in no time."

Mr. Willoughby flattened his ears and bared his teeth. "I am a peace-loving Home Tutor, but I'd advise you to remove your hand."

The teacher stepped back so fast, she nearly knocked Ms. Linden off her feet. "Very well," she snapped. "We'll see what the Administrator has to say about this."

All the teachers except Ms. Linden followed as she marched off. Her outraged voice floated back to us. "Unspeakable! Unethical! We must do something!"

Ms. Linden eyed the three of us clustered around Mr. Willoughby. "I'm glad to see you working to-

gether as a team. Don't worry, Tria, I'll make sure the Administrator investigates your mother's where-abouts." I flinched as she patted my shoulder and said good-bye.

Dayla kicked at the sand. "How will I convince my father to let me come home now?"

"We should never have come back," I cried. "We should have gone straight to town."

Mr. Willoughby pawed the ground. "We had to try for the car. And I was hoping someone would help us. But it's not too late. Let's go."

"I will come with you," Brash said, hopping onto his horse.

"I'm not going to chase after kidnappers and thieves! You'll be killed!" Dayla mounted her horse. "I'm going to the Residence Hall and take a shower."

I shrugged. "Suit yourself." I struggled onto Mr. Willoughby, and we headed for the front gate.

Suddenly the gate opened, and a baby blue con-vertible shot through. The top was down and the Administrator waved as he pulled to a stop.

"Isn't this car a gem? Are you the winning team? Congratulations!" Then he frowned. "But you can't get into my car looking like that. I just got it cleaned."

"They're losers!" Meta ran out of the Residence

Hall as Dayla changed course and galloped toward us. "My team won."

The Administrator shook his head. "No one here is a loser."

"Administrator!" Ms. Linden and the other teachers waved their arms and shouted. Their voices rose in a confusing babble.

"Come here, quick!"

"Robo horse!"

The Administrator popped open the door and dashed over to them. "What is it?" The teachers crowded around him, pushing and yelling.

Meta smirked at Dayla. "Knew you wouldn't win," she said in her shrill voice. "I'm surprised your team didn't run off and leave you."

Dayla sniffed and looked down her nose. "Is that what happened to you?"

Meta sputtered.

The sun was almost directly overhead. We had an air car and an open gate. "Mr. Willoughby, do you think you could fit in the back of that car?"

He cocked his head and studied the car. "Yes, but—"

Brash turned his glowing face to me. "Always I drive the farm tractor wishing it was a car." He climbed into the driver's seat, reached back, and opened the rear door. "Come on, Mr. Willoughby!"

"You can't do that!" Meta grabbed the door.

"Leave them alone," Dayla growled.

"We have to rescue my mom." I held the door, and Mr. Willoughby stepped in gingerly.

I started to slide into the smooth purple front seat, but Meta pulled me back. "Get out of there!"

Dayla sighed. "You'll never get anywhere without my help."

She pried Meta's fingers off my arm, and I jumped in beside Brash. "Go, Brash!"

The car lifted with a purr. At the last second, Dayla leaped into the backseat beside Mr. Willoughby. "You're going to need someone with brains," she muttered.

Meta covered her face as sand blew up around her. We zipped through the gate in the front wall, the Administrator yelling behind us, "My car! Come back!"

"This control panel shines!" Brash exclaimed. "This car is most well tended."

Dayla ran her hand over the door. "This old thing doesn't even have a communicator," she said in disgust.

I couldn't believe Brash and Dayla were helping

me! I looked at them, both covered in dirt and sand, and knew I'd never understand them the way I would a hologram. I smiled. It didn't matter.

"Do you know where you're going, Farm Boy?" Dayla asked as we headed out into the scrubby open countryside.

"I am homing in on the town beacon," Brash said confidently. "We have only a few minutes more."

We were going to be on time!

Something wet hit my nose. The sky had gone a smoky gray, and more wet things pelted my cheeks and face. I ducked.

"We're being attacked!"

Dayla laughed and turned her face upward. Drops of water beat down on her face. "It's raining, Fluff Brain. Haven't you ever seen rain before?"

"Of course I have," I said, hunching my shoulders. I didn't tell her I'd only seen it on holo vids. I'd never felt it thumping on my head, cold and wet and tickly where it ran down my neck.

"The Administrator will not like this." Brash looked uneasily at the water dripping on the air car's panels and seats. The dirt and sand from our clothes were smearing in filthy red streaks across the interior.

I wasn't worried about the car. "Will it hurt you,

Mr. Willoughby?" I leaned back and tried to shield him with my body.

"No." Mr. Willoughby shook his head, pelting me with water from his mane. "And the storm is already passing." He reached down and nosed my shoulder. "We have to make a plan."

Dayla dug into her pocket. "How about telling the kidnapper that this is the real device?" She opened her palm and I saw the pink rock.

"Perfect!" She handed it to me, and I stuck it in my pocket. A memory tickled the back of my brain. Something about the grayish pink wedge about the size of Star's thumb. But the thought slipped away before I could catch it.

Brash broke into my thoughts. "We must go with stealth and cunning."

"When we get to town, we'll split up," Dayla said, bossy as ever.

"I'll stay with Tria," Mr. Willoughby said. "You two take the car and follow us. Make sure you're not seen. Be ready to create a diversion if necessary."

Up ahead I saw a figure standing beside a big black air car, and my heart stood still.

"Look! It's Zell! We can get Star back!"

But as we got closer, I bit my lip in disappointment.

It wasn't Zell or Chip. A stout man in a brown and green uniform motioned for us to stop.

"A Planetary Guard!" Brash said. "He has a uniform like my brother's. He will help us." He cut the engine, and we glided down beside the guard.

I started talking fast. "My mother's been kidnapped, and we have to find her or they'll hurt her. A man called the Captain has her. They're hiding somewhere in town."

"Whoa," the guard said, with a pleased smile. "It's *your* mom who's been kidnapped by the Captain?" he asked me.

"Yes! It is quite true," Brash said, nodding several times.

"Call for help!" Dayla demanded.

"Oh, I'll call, all right," the guard said with that same smile. He murmured into his personal communicator. "Tria . . . three of them and a robo horse . . ."

A horrible realization hit me. I grabbed Dayla and Brash.

"He's one of the kidnappers," I whispered.

chapter seventeen

"**He is** not." Brash pulled away from me, with a superior look on his face. "He wears the uniform of a guard."

"Yeah, what's the matter with you, Fluff Brain?"

"He knows my name." I watched comprehension dawn on Brash's and Dayla's faces.

"What are we going to do?" Dayla blurted out.

"He knows where my mother is. I'll go with him. You go for help in town."

"I'm coming with you," whispered Mr. Willoughby.

I opened the back door, but the guard barked, "Hold it. Everyone stay in the car. My boss wants to talk to all of you. Follow me. Where'd you get that old car anyway?"

"This is bad," Dayla said uneasily. "Let's get out of here."

Brash shook his head. "His air car is much faster. He will catch us."

The guard led us away from town and across the red sand until we started to see hills in the distance.

"I believe we are headed for the sheerfaced hills. Uninhabited now, but the native people used to live in caves there." Mr. Willoughby narrowed and widened his eyes to focus better. "There's something on top of the cliffs. It looks like a car."

We heard a buzzing noise. Rising out of a clump of hazelite trees was a black air car with two big dents in the hood.

I pointed. "It's Zell and Chip!" We could rescue Star! "Go after them!"

But we didn't have to go after them. They headed straight for us. And rammed the Administrator's baby blue car.

Safety cushions immediately surrounded us, so I barely felt the impact. Then the cushions deflated and the front of the convertible burst into flames.

Dayla shouted, "Out, out, out!" and flung herself over the side of the car without opening the door. Brash jumped out behind her. He yanked open the back door. "Hurry, Mr. Willoughby!"

I clambered out, but Mr. Willoughby didn't move. The flames snapped and crackled. A plume of black smoke rose into the sky, and the smell of burning polymers stung my nose.

I reached back in and grabbed him around the neck. "Come on!"

Mr. Willoughby's deep voice was as calm as ever. "I seem to be stuck."

Brash and Dayla were right beside me. All three of us pulled and pushed. Mr. Willoughby didn't move.

"You kids get away from that car!" The guard came running over. "You're going to get hurt."

I wondered why he cared.

"He's right," said Mr. Willoughby. "You must stand back."

I shook my head and kept pulling. The flames were shooting higher, sending sparks flying onto the front seat. An ember landed on my arm. I brushed it away, but my skin kept burning.

"Throw sand on the flames! That will put them

out." Brash scooped up a hatful of sand and emptied it on the front of the car. Nothing happened. "More! More!" he shouted.

"Sensible boy." Mr. Willoughby nodded in approval. "That might work."

Dayla and I dashed to the front of the car and started dumping sand on it. The Guard took off his jacket, filled it with sand, and threw it on the car. Some of the flames sputtered and went out. Coughing and choking from the smoke, we buried the front of the car in sand until every flame was smothered.

I rushed back to examine Mr. Willoughby. "Are you all right?"

Mr. Willoughby tossed his head, and sand flew off him. "Sandy and slightly burned, but overall I am quite well. Thank you."

"You're welcome." I hugged him tight. Dayla and Brash, faces smudged with soot and sand, hugged him, too.

"You're crazy!"

I spun around to see the guard yelling at Zell and Chip. "I was just hired to take some kid out to the caves. No violence, I told them! Then you come along and ram the car. Are you insane?"

Zell smiled. "Perhaps you should leave while you still can."

The guard scooped up his jacket from the sand. "Come on, kids, get in my car."

Zell shook her head. "The kids stay."

"I won't be paid unless—"

Zell rested her hand on her weapon. The man looked at us, then hurried to his air car and drove away.

Zell and Chip walked toward us. "Tria, you have something I want, and I have something you want. Let's trade."

There was only one thing she had that I wanted: Star.

Chip was shaking his head at the smoking car. He turned to me. "I told you you'd be safer if you stayed away. See what happened? You might have been hurt."

"He has this goody-goody streak I can't seem to program out," Zell said in exasperation. She glared at me. "Nothing from that vase made Chip solid. You must have the real device. Give it to me, and I'll give you the disk."

Hadn't they found the wedge? "Give me Star first."

"No."

The sun was directly overhead. It was noon.

I needed to get to Mom. Maybe I could trick Zell into giving me Star, but it would take time and I didn't have any left. What was I going to do?

Zell's communicator beeped. "What?" She tipped her head and whispered to Chip. "It's that cursed Captain." She listened, frowning. "Yes, I have it. I have the girl, too. Very well." She waved at me. "Into the car. No, not you two," she scolded Brash and Dayla. "Just her."

My friends stood their ground. "No!"

I swallowed hard and said in a voice I hoped Zell and Chip couldn't hear, "Our plan, remember? We separate so you can make a diversion later."

Mr. Willoughby held onto my shirt with his teeth. "Let go!" I protested.

His mouth was full of cloth, and he had to let go of me to talk. "The plan was that I go with you."

I stroked his mane. "But you're stuck. Work on that diversion, okay?"

I walked over to Zell's car. She gave me a hard shove, and I tumbled into the backseat. I fell against the stuffed pillowcase with everything Zell had stolen from my pod. Zell and Chip jumped in after me.

Dayla's projector was on the front seat, and I grabbed for it.

"Naughty, naughty," Zell said, scooping it up. "Your precious Star isn't in there anyway."

"Where is she? What have you done with her?"

"She's all right," Chip whispered.

"Shut up." Zell glowered at him. Then she turned to me. "If you give me the device, I'll tell you where she is."

Could I fool her with the rock?

"We'd better hurry," Chip said. "The Captain is waiting."

"Captain schmaptain," Zell said, but she started the car.

We sputtered and buzzed toward the cliffs. I huddled on the seat, clinging to the thought that I'd soon see Mom.

The car spiraled higher and higher as we approached the cliffs. "Kid, this is your last chance." Zell reached into her shoe and pulled out a silver disk. She held it up for me to see.

"Tell me where the device is or you'll never see your friend again."

I lunged for the disk, but she jerked away. "I don't know! I swear I don't know."

"Too bad!" Zell said. She opened the window.

"Zell, no!" Chip and I cried at the same time.

Sunlight flashed on a small silver circle spinning through the sky.

Star was gone.

chapter eighteen

We landed with a series of clangs that reminded me of the Borgarian cymbal music Star liked. I choked back a sob. I wouldn't cry in front of Zell. And I *would* find Star. No matter what it took or how long I had to search, Star and I would be together again.

I clung to this thread of hope as the doors opened and Zell pushed me out. "You go first. Into that cave."

The cliff face jutted out over a small dark opening and sloped up to a mesa.

I shook my head. "There might be animals in there."

"There's something *worse* than animals." Zell shoved a lantern into my hands and grabbed the pillowcase and Chip's projector.

She pushed me in front of her. The cave was as dark as my pod had been the time I blew out all the power. Zell switched on the lantern and led the way to a cleft in the cave wall. I stumbled after her, up a passage that twisted and turned through the inside of the mountain. Finally we came out into a big cavern, lit by lanterns. In a flat space in the middle, a table was set up with tools. I saw a MegaWonderTool and magnifiers and piles of other equipment.

A man leaped out of the shadows, landed in a half crouch, and aimed a heavy-duty weapon at us. "Identify yourselves," he barked.

I shrank back, but Zell grabbed my arm before I could run.

"Shoo," she said, flapping a hand at the man. "Go tell the Captain we're here."

"I'm warning you—" He narrowed his eyes and raised the weapon.

"Stand down, soldier." The Captain strode from the back of the cavern, followed by a balding man whose eyes darted from Zell to me and back again.

The soldier instantly stood at attention and saluted smartly. "Sir! Yes Sir!"

"Turn him off, turn him off," the bald man said impatiently.

"Of course, Doctor." The Captain paused at the

table and fumbled among the instruments. The soldier—a hologram—disappeared.

The Doctor was staring at us with a fierce intensity. "Where's the device?" he demanded.

I yanked my arm out of Zell's grip. "Where's my mom?"

"The device is in here," Zell said, dramatically throwing the pillowcase on the table.

"Be careful!" The doctor's mouth went wide with horror, and he clutched at his tufts of white flyaway hair. He pushed past Zell and carefully pulled out components, laying them gently on the table. I watched but didn't see a pink wedge.

"Are you what I've been searching for?" The man clutched a cylinder tightly to his chest. "Once I figure out how you work, I'll copy you. We'll make all my soldiers solid. We'll build armies of holograms, construct hologram cities, and *zap!* they'll be real." His voice rose to a feverish pitch. "We'll be more powerful than anyone else in the galaxy."

"Easy, Dr. Roparian." The Captain put a hand on the man's shoulder. "Let's make sure we have the right one before we get carried away."

Dr. Roparian sighed and carefully laid the cylinder on the table. The Captain turned to us. His nose ring glinted in the lantern light.

"Thank you, Zell and Chip. As soon as we've verified it's here, you'll be paid."

Zell stepped up until she was nose to nose with the Captain.

"Pay us now. And a bonus for bringing the kid."

"What do you think, Dr. Roparian?" the Captain said without taking his eyes off Zell.

Dr. Roparian was examining the cylinder, zapping it and testing it with his instruments. Suddenly he smashed it against the rock floor. "It's nothing but a residence cleaner transfer tube." He gripped the MegaWonderTool in clawlike fingers and advanced on Zell. "You're trying to trick us."

"You're crazy!" She jumped out of his way and pointed at me. "She knows which is the real one."

I edged away, watching the doctor warily as he spun toward me. "Maybe I do," I said. "And maybe it's not any of those."

"Doctor, calm down." The Captain stepped between us. "Tria, give me the device, and I promise the Doctor won't hurt you." He glared at the Doctor.

"Give the device to me," Zell said, pulling out her blaster. "I need it for Chip."

I stared at them, my heart pounding. The Doctor with his zapping MegaWonderTool, Zell with her blaster, and the Captain. They were all crazy. "Where's my mother?" I shouted.

"We don't have time for this." Dr. Roparian turned off the MegaWonderTool, smoothed his few wisps of hair, wiggled his jaw, and rolled his head from side to side. He sucked in a great breath of air, held it, and blew it out again. "There, that's better. Captain, pay Zell and get her out of here." His voice snapped with authority.

"Very well, Doctor. Account number?" The Captain raised his eyebrows at Zell.

The Captain wasn't in charge, I realized. This crazy doctor was.

Zell holstered her weapon and rattled off a string of numbers, and the Captain relayed them to his communicator. "It's done. Go."

"But you said we'd test the device on Chip."

"Go." The Captain placed a hand on his blaster.

Zell fingered her own weapon and looked at Chip.

"Go, or I'll get Gralog."

Zell and Chip immediately fled down the passageway.

Who was Gralog? Anyone who could scare Zell had to be terrifying.

"This isn't over," Zell called over her shoulder, with

a special glare for me. "I'll be back. Chip deserves to be solid."

"Where's my device?" Dr. Roparian growled.

I had to come up with a way to delay him. I pulled out the pink rock. "This is an essential part of the device. But you need to put it together properly. And I'm not going to tell you which piece it goes with until you take me to my mother."

Gingerly the Doctor took the rock and nodded at the Captain. "Take her back." He twitched his mouth at me. "You'd better be telling us the truth. Or you and your mother will be sorry."

I gulped. Mom and I would have to escape fast.

The Captain led me down a dark passage that shimmered with nightglows. I stumbled on the rough rock and grabbed at the wall for balance. It was sharp and jagged. And it dripped.

"Ugh." I wiped my hand on my pant leg.

Something growled in the darkness.

"What was that?"

The Captain drew his blaster. "Gralog. He's a bit crazed from the heat, but he's a good guard. Good boy, Gralog," he said in a soothing tone. In the shadows ahead I made out a massive form low to the ground, hackles rising and small pointed ears flat to its head.

Sharp teeth gleamed in the nightglow light. It was covered in thick, shiny black hair. Gralog was an animal! I froze.

"Good boy." The Captain reached out and seized the beast by the chain around its short, thick neck. The other end of the chain was bolted to the rock wall. Behind him I saw the entrance to another cave. "Your mother's in there."

"Mom?" I called anxiously.

My mother rushed to the cave opening. The blood drained from her face when she saw me. "Tria! What are you doing here?"

It was really her! I edged along the wall, keeping the Captain between me and Gralog, and dashed into the cave. "Mom!" I hugged her tight, and she squeezed me back. "Are you okay?"

"I'm fine. How about you?" She pushed me away, studied my face, and pulled me into another hug.

"Zell threw Star out of the air car. She's lost in the sand." All the overwhelming feelings of loss and rage I'd felt when Zell first took Star flooded over me again.

Mom's arms tightened around me. "We'll get her back." Her voice was tough and determined and pushed away my tidal wave of grief. "We'll get her back," she repeated.

"Very touching." I turned to see the Captain still clutching the beast's chain. Its small brown eyes glared, and drool dripped from its open mouth. "Now tell me what the other piece looks like."

Mom looked at me questioningly. I didn't meet her eyes as I swiftly thought back to the components I'd shoved into the Olympian vase. My reply had to be complicated enough to keep the Doctor busy for a while. "It's a segmented cylinder," I said slowly. "With an elbow joint near the top third segment."

Without a word, the Captain released the beast and rushed down the passage.

"We have to get out of here. It won't take him long to figure out I was describing the bioregulator from our atmosphere controller," I blurted out.

Mom had tears in her eyes. "Tria, I am so proud of you. You're Outside. And there's even an animal here, and you're not panicking." She grabbed me and hugged me again. "You must have so much to tell me."

"Mom! We don't have time for this. We have to escape."

She shook her head. I saw one filigree earring swinging against her cheek, and I was reminded of the Captain's threats. "Honey, there's no way out. Except past that beast."

Uh-oh. "No tiny passages in the back?"

Mom shook her head.

"No holes in the ceiling or floor?"

"I've searched. The beast guards the only way out."

I shuddered and carefully didn't look at the drooling creature and his dagger sharp teeth. "Maybe we can get past him." A lot of things I'd thought were scary turned out to be things I could handle. Maybe Gralog was another of them. I made myself look at him.

His head was small and narrow, ending in a moist black nose on a pointed snout. His powerfully built body and muscular legs were covered with masses of dense black hair.

At least his hair is pretty, I told myself.

My eyes met his, and suddenly Gralog spun around, flattening his ears and growling. I jumped back, breaking out in a cold sweat. But he wasn't growling at me. Someone was coming down the passage.

"Stay back," Mom said, shoving me behind her.

Dr. Roparian charged into view. "It's a fake! Where's the real one?"

"Doctor, wait," the Captain shouted from down the passage. "The beast!"

Gralog leaped. He clamped his sharp teeth on the Doctor's arm and didn't let go.

The Doctor screamed and stumbled backward,

trying to push the animal away with his other arm, but Gralog clung to him.

I stared in fascination at Gralog's teeth.

"Doctor!" The Captain was getting closer.

"Come on!" Mom tugged my arm, and we dashed past Dr. Roparian and Gralog. Mom turned to the right, away from the Captain's advancing footsteps.

We bumped into the walls as we raced along, unable to see as the nightglows faded behind us. I hoped we'd end up on top of the cliffs where Mr. Willoughby thought he'd spotted a car.

It was getting lighter. There was an opening up ahead. "It's the way out!" I cried.

We dashed to the opening and skidded to a halt. Mom flung out her arm to keep me back, and we stood staring out at the ground far, far below. There were no ledges or paths.

Mom and I stared at each other. "What are we going to do?" My chest was heaving, and I knew I couldn't run any farther.

"We'll rest a moment, then search for the passage to the top of the cliff." Mom gasped out the words.

Across the scrubby sand, I saw a blue dot with a thin trail of smoke rising above it.

"Look, Mom." I pointed. "I came in that car with my friends and Mr. Willoughby."

Mom squinted. "That car is smoking." Then her eyes popped wide. "Did you say Mr. Willoughby?"

"Yes." I felt my face turn red. "I accidentally put him into your old robo horse."

"Tria, no!"

"But he likes it. Look, what's that?"

We watched a dusty shape race across the sand toward us. I wished for Mr. Willoughby's telescopic vision. "Maybe it's someone coming to rescue us," I said. And then, as it came closer, I shouted, "It's Dayla and Brash on Mr. Willoughby!" I grabbed Mom's arm and jumped up and down. "I wonder how they freed Mr. Willoughby."

"Freed him from what?"

"It happened when the cars crashed and we caught on fire." I saw Mom's face and shut my mouth abruptly. "I'll tell you later. Brash! Dayla! We're up here!" But they couldn't hear me. I watched as they surveyed the cliff. Then they slid off Mr. Willoughby and darted forward.

"They've found the entrance," I said. They pointed and gestured, and I realized Mr. Willoughby was probably trying to talk them out of going in. "I'm not sure if that's good or bad."

"Bad," said the Captain's voice behind us. "Very, very bad."

Mom and I spun to face him. My heart, already

161

pounding hard, gave an extra big leap when I saw the blaster in his hand. He motioned us away from the opening. "Now let's see who's out there." Keeping the blaster trained on us, he looked out and down.

"More kids." He shrugged. "I'll deal with them later. I'll just get rid of their means of escape."

Mom had pushed me behind her, but I could still see out. The Captain took quick aim and fired. Down on the sand Mr. Willoughby sparkled and slowly collapsed in a heap.

chapter nineteen

Mom and I stood side by side next to the table of instruments. I scarcely noticed the holo projector sitting there. I held Mom's hand tightly, feeling like I'd been hit by a stunner. I couldn't believe it. Again and again I saw Mr. Willoughby sparkle and fall. Every circuit, every connection and component must have been blasted to a melted ruin. First I'd lost Star, and now Mr. Willoughby. I was losing everyone I cared about. I gripped Mom's hand hard.

"Where is the device?" The Captain pointed his weapon, first at Mom, then at me.

Mom pressed her lips together and shook her head.

Dr. Roparian shifted impatiently, cradling his injured arm to his chest. Bloodstained bandages wound unevenly from his wrist to his elbow. I wondered what they'd done with the beast.

When we didn't answer, Dr. Roparian snatched the blaster from the Captain. "Tell us!" He fired at the ground, and the rocks exploded. Mom and I dived behind the table as shards ricocheted around us. Outside, something crashed and thudded down the cliff face.

"You fool!" The Captain wrestled the weapon away from the Doctor. "You're going to cause a rock slide and we'll all be buried in here."

"It's worth the risk." Dr. Roparian's mouth twitched. "Making a hologram solid is worth anything."

The Captain holstered the blaster. Gently he put his hands on the Doctor's shoulders and turned him around. "I promise I'll get the device," he said soothingly. "Why don't you go over to the passageway and make sure those kids aren't coming?"

I hoped Brash and Dayla were safely away from there.

They weren't.

"Everyone stay where you are!" Dayla marched into the cavern with her pop gun pointed at the Doctor. Brash followed, turning off his candle as he entered.

Their grimy faces were streaked with tears, but Dayla's mouth was firm and Brash's brow furrowed in determination.

The men froze.

"Let's go, Fluff Brain," Dayla said. She would have sounded tough except that her voice trembled.

Mom and I edged around the table toward Dayla.

"It's just a propulsion gun!" The Doctor made a sudden swipe and jerked the pop gun out of Dayla's hand. He held it up to his ear and shook it. "Empty, too, by the sound of it." He laughed, aimed it at the top of the cavern, and pulled the trigger.

The gun discharged with a loud *pop!* Something smashed into the ceiling. A torrent of rocks and splinters rained down on us.

I snatched up the soldier's holo projector as Mom and I dashed toward Brash, Dayla, and the passageway. The rock storm got worse. Boulders bounced off walls. Lanterns smashed to the ground. I lost Mom in a dark nightmare of crashing rocks.

"Doctor! This way!" the Captain shouted from the back of the cavern.

"My device—" The thunder of falling rocks covered Dr. Roparian's words. Then I heard the Captain again.

"—go to the air car."

I hoped Gralog would get them. A chunk of rock crashed beside me, and I hurled myself out of the way, huddling against a wall until only pebbles slid and bounced around. As the dust cleared, a small light shone in the cavern. Brash placed his candle on top of a boulder. He seemed to be in one piece.

"Mom?" I stood slowly, muscles trembling, clutching the projector to my chest. "Mom?" There was no answer. Frantically I scrambled over heaps of fallen rocks. "Mom!"

As I scraped past a boulder, I spotted Dayla, rolling rocks out of the way and calling, "Mom!" She caught my eye and smiled weakly. "I don't know her name."

Brash yelled, "She is here."

Mom lay against a big boulder. Her eyes were closed, her body limp. I remembered the robo horse's body before I activated it. "She's not dead," I whispered. "Not dead."

"Her pulse is strong," Brash said, holding Mom's wrist.

She was alive! Tears of relief streamed down my face. I took Mom's hand in mine and knelt beside her.

"Now what?" Dayla asked.

Rubble and boulders filled the cavern around us. There was no sign of the men, the beast, or the passage.

I shoved the projector at Dayla. "Here. You can have Benjamin back."

Brash's eyes widened. "Zell returned Star!"

I shook my head. I didn't want to talk about Star yet. "It's the Doctor's projector. I couldn't let his hologram soldier be buried forever. Go ahead, Dayla, use it for Benjamin."

"Thanks, Fluff Brain." She looked at me thoughtfully. "But I don't think Benjamin would like it in here. I'll wait till we're in the sunshine." She shrugged off her dirty daypack and stuffed the projector inside.

"We will get Star back," Brash told me softly.

"Star—" I began, and then noticed a triangular orange head poking out of a torn box on his survival belt. Four webbed feet and a slender body quickly followed.

"Brash!" I screamed.

His hand flew to his waist, but he was too late. The coral spud jumped onto a nearby rock and darted into a crevice.

"Do not be fearful," he said, anxiously watching me. "He is harmless."

"Of course it's harmless." Dayla frowned. "It's only a coral spud."

The coral spud stuck its head out of the crevice and zipped over to Dayla. She laughed. "Come here, little thing."

But it dodged around her and jumped onto my shoe. My heart gave a great thump of fear.

"Easy." Brash inched toward us. "I will catch him."

I didn't care what anyone else said. I knew that if I moved, the coral spud would bite me and I would die. The coral spud looked up at me and blinked. Its gaze shifted to Mom, and I felt my heart beat again, fast and furious. The spud was going to bite Mom! Blood thundered through my veins and lightning bolts of energy zapped me into action.

"Stay away from my mom!" I yelled, sweeping my hand toward the coral spud. It skittered away and disappeared behind a far rock.

"He was a pet." Brash sighed and fingered the torn box. "But now he is free, and that is better."

I stared in disbelief at the rock where the coral spud had disappeared. I was still alive—and so was Mom! I was panting as if I had just run a race.

"Brash, shine your light over there," Dayla said suddenly. "I think that's where the passage was."

Brash swung his light. "Yes! Help me move this boulder."

Dayla and Brash put their shoulders against the boulder and pushed. It rocked but didn't move.

"Help us, Fluff Brain!"

"No. I'm not leaving Mom." I glared at the place where the coral spud had disappeared. "That spud might come back."

Brash shook his head. "Spuds do not like noise and activity. He will hide now. Your mother is safe, and we need your help."

I held Mom's limp hand and considered. We had to get out of here. And what Brash said made sense.

We shoved and pushed and managed to roll the huge rock to the side. Brash shined his light over the knee-high rocks that were still left. "Yes! It is the passage!"

A low, dark form rose out of the shadows, teeth bared and growling.

We'd found Gralog.

"It is a furbeast!" Brash cried. He leaned over with his hand out. I pulled him back just as the animal snapped at him.

"Gralog is a very mean furbeast," I warned anxiously.

"Furbeasts are not mean." Brash was furious.

"Who has done this?" He pointed at the broken chain dangling from the animal's neck. "And he has been hurt!" A streak of matted hair and blood ran across the creature's back.

"Tria?"

I spun around. "Mom!"

She was trying to sit up, lines of pain etched on her face. "I'm okay," she whispered. She rubbed her forehead. "Took a knock on the head, that's all." She tried to stand but collapsed. "And a sprained ankle, I think."

"Don't worry. We'll take care of you," I promised, choking back tears.

Dayla put her pack under Mom's ankle. "It helps to elevate it. Brash, what else do you do for a sprained ankle?"

He left the furbeast and searched his belt. I kept watch behind him, hoping the low rock wall would keep Gralog away from us.

"We should bind it up," Brash said. "But I do not have any long cloths." He pulled out a handful of water bubbles and offered them to Mom. She took three, giving him a grateful smile.

Dayla bent forward so her hair hid her face. It wasn't bright krylar yellow anymore. Now it was more of a dirty sandy brown. She pulled Benjamin's bag from the pack under Mom's foot, unwrapped Benjamin, and handed the cloth to Brash. Then she stuffed the disk into her shoe.

I cleared my throat. "Thanks, Dayla."

Brash bandaged Mom's ankle while she watched him through half-closed eyes.

"We need to get out of here before the Captain comes back." I stood. "One of us has to get past that animal and go for help."

"I'm a good runner," Dayla said.

Mom blinked several times. "Tria, I don't think—"

I rummaged through my pack. "Food!" I held up a peanut butter sandwich. I tore it apart and gave Brash half. "Brash and I will distract Gralog with the sandwich, and Dayla can slip past while he's eating it."

Mom rubbed her forehead and frowned. "I don't know . . ."

"We can do it." I hoped I sounded braver than I felt.

The three of us returned to the knee-high rock wall. The furbeast growled, lips raised over sharp teeth, saliva dripping down his chin.

"He is overheated. He should have been clipped by now," Brash said indignantly.

I wanted to drop the sandwich and run into the

darkest corners of the cave. I wanted to curl up in a little ball until everyone and everything went away.

I have faced a coral spud, I reminded myself.

"Let's do this." Dayla leaned forward, ready to run.

"Do not run. We must be slow and friendly," Brash said. "It's okay, Gralog. Here is food." Slowly he stretched out his hand, holding the sandwich in his fingertips. The animal pricked his ears and reached toward Brash with his teeth showing. I started shaking. This was a bad idea. I remembered how the doctor screamed when Gralog's teeth sank into his arm.

Before I could say anything, Gralog pulled the sandwich away from Brash and swallowed it in one quick gulp. Then he nosed Brash's hand and looked hopefully up at him. Brash gently rolled him the rest of the water bubbles. Gralog ate them so fast I doubted he even tasted the water.

"Tria. Give him your sandwich."

Give it to him? I'd planned on *throwing* it at him. "Good Gralog," I croaked. I stuck my shaking hand out, but when he looked at me, I quickly dropped the sandwich and snatched my hand back. Gralog snapped the food off the ground and ate it whole.

"He should be friendly now." Brash slowly stepped over the low wall. The beast perked his ears at Brash and wagged his stubby tail.

I let out my breath and heard a whoosh as Dayla did the same.

"If you move slowly and quietly, we can leave." Brash laid a gentle hand on the animal's head. "Gralog and I will lead the way. We must get healing cloths for him."

"You start ahead. We'll follow you."

Dayla and I helped Mom over the low wall and supported her as she limped down the rough passageway. Brash carried the candle and coaxed Gralog to lumber along beside him. The furbeast turned to look at us, but Brash spoke soothingly, and they walked on together. We hadn't gone far when I heard a clumping and banging ahead.

"Something is there," Brash whispered. "Something big!"

Gralog flattened his ears and growled.

"Maybe the Captain is coming back for us!" Swiftly I bent and scooped up a handful of rocks. "Mom can't run. We'll have to fight."

The noise came closer.

None of us moved. At that moment I knew I had

friends to be proud of. I held my rocks ready and watched the passage as the noises grew louder.

Tiny twin beams of light shot around the curve.

"There you are," a deep calm voice said. "Is everyone all right?"

chapter twenty

The creature with the glowing eyes lowered his head to touch noses with the furbeast.

"Mr. Willoughby!"

I dropped the rocks and ran for him. "You're alive!"

I hugged him, Brash thumped him on the shoulder, and Dayla patted his nose. "Have you noticed my headlight eyes?" he asked proudly. "I also have a sonar, probably from the Fly-by-night, but I'm more accustomed to feedback from visual circuits, so I used the headlight beams."

"They're wonderful," I said into his mane. "Just wonderful."

"Mr. Willoughby?" Mom hopped forward. "We thought you were dead."

"Allow me to carry you," Mr. Willoughby said. "And I'll explain as we go."

We helped Mom scramble onto his back. "Keep your head down," I warned. "The ceiling gets low in places." Mom smiled at me as I walked beside her and Mr. Willoughby. I had them both back! I couldn't believe it. If only I had Star, too.

"Why aren't you blasted to bits?" Dayla demanded. "We saw you get hit."

Mr. Willoughby trembled all over and I stroked his neck. "It was very strange. I felt something hit me and I fell, but the blast went straight through me. Like I wasn't solid at all."

"Most marvelous," Brash said solemnly.

"What else did you mix into him, Fluff Brain?"

I thought. "Maybe the atmosphere controller and the ball-a-rang, and . . ." I trailed off. "But there's nothing that makes a blast pass right through you like you're not even solid."

I heard what I'd just said. "Oh!" Suddenly I remembered where I'd seen a grayish pink wedge.

"I put the pink wedge into Mr. Willoughby," I said in awe.

Dayla gasped. "Fluff Brain! You didn't!"

"And I helped!" Brash hit his forehead with his hand. "Now I remember."

"Most interesting." Mr. Willoughby continued to

step carefully along. "And somehow, instead of making holograms solid, it made me into a hologram when I got hit with a blaster."

I shook my head in wonder. "We've been looking for it all this time and it's been in Mr. Willoughby!"

"Perhaps I can access it."

Everyone was so quiet I could hear Gralog's nails clicking as he walked over the rocks. Suddenly I pictured what would happen if Mr. Willoughby became a hologram. I turned to catch Mom, who would fall if he did.

But he stayed solid. "No, I can't locate it."

"No one else must know where the device is," Mom said, her voice low and intent.

"I promise!" Brash said quickly.

Dayla echoed him. "I'll never tell."

With a device like that, I could make Star solid. But that wasn't Star's dream, and I finally decided it wasn't mine either. If I ever got Star back, I'd let her be herself.

"I promise, too," I said.

Ahead of us the darkness was getting lighter. We walked out of the cave and stood blinking in the brightness.

Mom grinned down at me. "You found an excellent hiding place for the device."

"Shhh!" I glanced quickly around. No sign of the Captain or the Doctor. "Mr. Willoughby, is anyone else out here?"

Dayla and Brash stood tensely beside me. Mom sat stiffly on Mr. Willoughby's back as his nostrils flared and his ears flipped back and forth. "We are alone."

Whew. Safe for now.

"I hope those men are squashed," Dayla said, pounding one fist into her palm.

Mom gave her a startled glance. "They probably got away. But we'll report them as soon as we get back to the school."

"My brother and the other Planetary Guards will catch them." Brash watched Gralog scurry around sniffing bushes and trees. He reached into his survival belt and pulled out a small pair of clippers. "Now I will make Gralog comfortable."

"No." My voice came out louder than I intended. I swallowed and went on more quietly. "Now we have to find Star. Zell threw her out of the car."

Mr. Willoughby gasped.

Dayla's hands clenched into fists. "That worm head."

I gulped. "We were close to the cliff, but I'm not sure where. Will you help me look?"

"We will find her," Brash said stoutly. "Furbeasts are good trackers. Perhaps Gralog will help."

"Wait!" Mr. Willoughby commanded before we could run off in all directions. "Don't stir up the sand. I'll look first."

We waited while Mr. Willoughby scanned the sand. He stepped in a small half-circle, pivoting slowly, examining the entire area.

Finally he shook his head. "I am sorry, Tria. I do not see a disk anywhere. But I cannot see through the bushes and trees, or over the mounds where the land rises."

Gralog lay panting in the scant shade of a scrubby tree. He would be no help.

"You are looking on the ground, Mr. Willoughby," Brash said slowly. "But maybe the disk did not fall all the way to the ground."

I frowned. How could it not fall all the way?

"Disks don't fly, Farm Boy," Dayla said.

"I know that," Brash said with dignity. "But perhaps it landed on the mountain."

I gasped and turned to look at the cliff. It was possible!

"You are a very smart boy," Mom said. "Do you see anything, Mr. Willoughby?"

"I'll have to move away to get a good view."

We trudged through the sand several hundred meters from the cliff. Mr. Willoughby scanned methodically side to side, top to bottom. "The air car is gone from the top of the mountain. And I don't see Star."

I sagged.

"Look, Tria, there's a bird," Mom called softly to me. "Wouldn't Star love it?"

I lifted my head to see a black bird with gleaming iridescent wings flying in tight circles over the cliff. As I watched, it spiraled lazily down and settled on the rocks.

"That's a filcher!" I cried. "They love shiny objects. Isn't that right, Mr. Willoughby?"

His voice lost its habitual calmness. "I think you've found her!"

The next second, we were all racing to the mountain with the furbeast loping after us. The bird took fright and flapped away.

We reached the bottom of the cliff, and Dayla said, "But if Star *is* there, how will we get her down? Mr. Willoughby, can you fly up there?"

Mr. Willoughby shook his head. "I can only float a few centimeters off the ground. But it's not far for a climber. I will guide Tria on the best route."

"Right," I said. I was already examining the cliff face for handholds.

"You?" Brash and Dayla stared at me in astonishment.

"Are you sure you can do this?" Mom asked. "I've always wanted you to go Outside, but I didn't mean for you to climb mountains on your first time out."

"Outside's not so bad. And I can do this. At least it's not raining, and no one is shooting at us." I looked hastily around to make sure this was true. "This is nothing compared to the Cliffs of Redvor!"

And it wasn't. The cliff face slanted inward slightly, so I didn't have to pull myself straight up but could climb and push easily.

"A little to your right, Tria, you're almost there!" Mr. Willoughby called.

I climbed with confidence and energy. I wished for gloves to protect my hands from the sharp rocks, but the small nicks and cuts were nothing if I could get Star back. At one point something darted past me on the rock face but I didn't even pause. Racknid or coral spud or unknown creature—it didn't matter. I only cared about reaching Star.

"Go, Tria!" Brash called.

"You can do it, Fluff Brain!"

I heard a thundering and glanced over my shoulder. A cloud of dust was moving toward us over the sand. I stiffened, fingers tightening on the rocks, toes wedged in crevices.

"It's the teachers," Mr. Willoughby called up to me. "They are on robo horses."

"They're coming to our rescue," Mom said, breaking into a smile.

Mr. Willoughby's ears flicked back and forth. "Not exactly. I can hear the Administrator shouting, 'My car! What have you done to my car?' "

I giggled and relaxed for a moment against the rock face. It wasn't really funny, of course. But it was much better than a sandstorm or criminals with blasters.

A moment later, I found Star nestled in a hollow between two rocks. Gently I scooped up the silver disk and tucked it into my pocket. Before I climbed down I paused for a moment, feeling the sun on my face and the wind in my hair. I didn't care if Star was solid or not. Just as long as we were together.

When I reached the ground, Dayla was waiting with the projector. Brash reached over and took the soldier's disk from the projection slot. "I will stick it in my shoe," he said with a grin.

Star's disk clicked sweetly into place, and I activated the projector.

"Star!" I was so happy to see her that even the Borgarian outfit looked good to me.

182

"Hi!" she said. Then she saw Mom and grinned from ear to ear. "You're safe!"

"Good to see you, Star," Mom said. "Have you been studying Borgar, by any chance?"

Star laughed and spun in a circle so Mom could admire her outfit from all sides.

"Star, guess what?" I broke in. "Zell threw you out of the air car, and I had to climb the mountain to rescue you!"

Star's eyes grew round. "You did? And what happened to the device?"

"I hid it," I said smugly.

"Yeah, wait till you hear where Fluff Brain put it," Dayla said.

My face got hot, and I didn't feel smug anymore.

Star winked at me, and immediately I felt better. "I'm sure Tria found an ingenious hiding place."

"She did," Brash said. "We have had many adventures. We were in a cave-in and a fire and—" He stopped as Mom gasped and looked uneasily at me.

"The important thing to remember, Mom," I said quickly, "is that we rescued you and Star and the device."

"You saved Outside, Tria," Mom said, gathering us all in a sandy hug. "You and your friends saved the world."

183

"And everything turned out fine," Mr. Willoughby said softly.

I felt a warm glow of satisfaction as I realized their words were true.

Mission accomplished.

about the author

Rebecca Kraft Rector is a children's librarian whose work has been published in several magazines for young readers. She wrote this book surrounded by photographs of her Earthbound family and friends, and received inspiration from her cat and horse. She lives with her husband in Monrovia, Maryland. *Tria and the Great Star Rescue* is her first novel. She has several copies on disk just to be safe.